HORSE POWER

Also by Rae D'Arcy

Hoof Beats

HORSE POWER

By

Rae D'Arcy

Order this book online at www.trafford.com
or email orders@trafford.com

Most Trafford titles are also available at major online book retailers.

Printed in the United States of America.

ISBN: 978-1-4269-4663-9 (sc)
ISBN: 978-1-4269-4662-2 (e)

Trafford rev. 12/10/2010

 www.trafford.com

North America & international
toll-free: 1 888 232 4444 (USA & Canada)
phone: 250 383 6864 ♦ fax: 812 355 4082

Acknowledgments

Thanks to: Patty, Arielle and Kathy for proofing
Kristen B for all her helpful hints
Kathy D for being my cheerleader

Cover design by Darcy Miller

CHAPTER ONE

I closed the door and leaned back against it. Before me was an empty apartment; neutral colored walls and carpet, like my life had become; empty and dull. My still-rolled sleeping bag lay on the living room floor. My suit cases were sitting in the corner. I had filled the cupboards with food but there was no can opener, plates or silver ware.

I had a week before I started my new job as executive secretary at the Hartman attorney-at-law office. I hadn't worked since my marriage to Josh ten years ago. Now divorced, I was hoping my knowledge, skills and confidence would return fast enough for me to hold onto this self-sustaining employment.

With my back to the door, I slid down to the variegated brown tiled kitchen floor; sat with my knees drawn up, hugging them, forehead resting on their knobbiness. I was again shocked and ashamed of how I had let Josh control and demolish the person I had once been, just because I thought I couldn't live without him.

I recalled the day, not so long ago, that, in a moment of rebellion I went to see an old friend. Josh had always demanded I was never to go to see Angel. How exhilarating it felt to defy him. There she suggested we go riding. It was something I once loved to do, but the sight of fiery steeds prancing in eagerness now terrified me. She had no placid mounts, only fiery steeds.

Angel was shocked at my timidity. "You need to dump Josh and become you again," she had claimed.

It was a seed sown. I dwelt on it; watered it with memories of what I was before I had let Josh take over my life. The brightness of the realization that I missed the old me nourished the seed like sunshine. Still, because I had fallen so far from my star, it took awhile to build up enough anger to run for my life. Even then, it took Angel's hand in mine pulling me along. She found the job opening in far away Montaine. She stood by me as I made the phone call from her home to arrange an interview. She encouraged me through the interview and cheered the successful job offer. She convinced me I needed a horse to aid me in the journey back to me. She had just acquired a horse that didn't measure up to her expectations and pretty much coerced me into accepting him at a diminished price. She even located a boarding stable just outside of town where I could keep CastleontheHudson.

So I would never have to see Josh again, I had taken a lump sum as my divorce settlement which Angel freely used to buy me a car, a few pieces of furniture, the fiery steed Hudson, and paid for a year's worth of boarding for him. Even now, he should be in his new home as I was in mine.

Angel had shown me the way to my place. We had cleaned it together with the smell of cleansers and disinfectants filling the air, scouring out my old life of dependency on a man. She helped me shop for groceries and wanted to purchase my dinnerware.

"No way. You've done enough for me already, Angel. I'll need something to do this week."

"You'll have plenty to do with Hudson. You'll love him. He's a great horse."

She brought in two boxes. The first I opened was a phone.

"You call me anytime, you hear?"

I smiled for the first time in a long time.

"The other box you are not permitted to open until you have shelves set up and at least your first book purchased. You always loved reading."

With a shock, I realized even that had fallen by the wayside as I had lost me.

I had a week to get set up before reporting to work. I knew I needed to start getting to know Hudson but it seemed all beyond my capabilities. I felt I was in way over my head. Angel had left and my resolve seemed to have left with her. I unrolled my sleeping bag, crawled in fully clothed and cried myself to sleep.

My first thought upon waking was to go introduce myself to Hudson but I decided to go shopping instead. I found a pay phone and called for phone service. By noon I had dinnerware, cookware, a can opener, a set of shelves which were still in the box needing assembled and had even purchased my first two books.

My furniture was supposed to arrive Tuesday morning, so to avoid going to see Hudson, I assembled the shelves and set my two books on it. I opened Angel's second gift which was horse-head book ends. I guiltily thought of Hudson, big and fiery, and went to the park.

It was spring. Kids were still in school, the pool not yet open. Only a few women were power walking on the paved jogging path or playing with pre-schoolers on swings, slides, and teeter-totters. I walked the streets and found specialty stores, a veterinarian's clinic and Grandma's café close to where I'd be working. Back at my apartment, the horse-head book ends accused me of neglecting Hudson. I called Angel and got her answering machine.

"I got my phone hooked up. 780-893-2428. Also got my shelves and two books. Thanks for the book ends...and for rescuing me. Catch you later."

A knock at the door early Tuesday morning got me moving. The furniture! I yelled "Just a minute," jumped into sweats forgoing the bra. For the first time I wondered what Angel had picked out for me; red and gold for the living room; midnight blue and crème for the bedroom. There were enough rugs to almost obliterate the beige carpet. She had even taken window measurements and purchased curtains and drapes.

As I looked around for the windows to match the curtains, I realized I had French doors opening out onto a balcony. How had I not noticed such a charming feature of my little place? I went out and looked down the tree-lined street and watched a jogger pass on the sidewalk beneath me. I smiled as I became aware for the first time of birdsong. I took a deep breath of damp, cool morning air. It would be a perfect time for a ride. I pictured Hudson in his new home waiting, wondering who his new owner was. Was he bewildered by why he was sent away? You're anthropomorphizing, I chided myself and went back inside.

Angel had purchased just enough to not overcrowd my small apartment. Even the desk and computer fit neatly in the bedroom. She had suggested an on-line refresher course. I installed internet and went shopping for something to cover the dull walls.

The rest of the week was spent on strolls around town, reading, and hours of studying the refresher material. I found a fitness club and joined. It would get me ready for riding, I reasoned.

Monday I reported to work, and worked out at the fitness club afterwards.

Wednesday evening the phone rang. The noise startled me into a jump. For a moment I wondered where it was coming from.

"Hello?"

"Jules, why haven't you been out to see Hudson?" Angel's voice was angry. "The stable manager called. They're wondering if he's stolen! He's getting hard to handle from lack of exercise. You get your butt out there. I didn't sell you that horse for him to be abused."

"I'm sorry Angel. I just haven't had time…."

"You take time! And give them your phone number. I don't want another one of those phone calls."

"I will."

There was a pause. "Are you okay, Jules?"

I smiled. That was the Angel I needed. "Just fearful and overwhelmed."

"Jump in with both feet Jules. If you can't swim, thrash your way."

"I think Hudson is too much horse for me."

"Jules, at least lunge him and groom him. Start getting to know him. He's not near as exuberant as the ones you used to ride."

"I know, but I'm not that person anymore."

"Yes you are. You're just hiding. When you were bold, Josh probably withheld affection, so you buried your self esteem."

I was silent as I realized that was exactly what had happened.

"Am I right?"

"Yes." It was almost a whisper.

"Do you still have the stable phone number?"

"Yes."

"Call them right now. Tell them you'll be out there after work tomorrow. And then BE THERE."

"I will."

"Hang in there Jules. You WILL get through this. You will be so happy when you've reclaimed yourself."

"Thanks for calling Angel."

As promised, I immediately called Phoenix stables. "Hello, this is Jewel Fitzgerald. I own CastleontheHudson."

"Hello. I'm glad you called. I'm Shelly the barn manager. Your friend said you're new to the area and are feeling a bit overwhelmed but you really need to come spend time with your horse. He's feeling abandoned. He's getting lots of attention from the stable hands but he'll be bonding with others if you don't come let him know you're the other part of the team. Arielle, one of the stable hands, started lunging him yesterday. He was getting very unruly. Turn out isn't enough exercise. I know you didn't request anyone to do that but I'd suggest you offer to pay her for doing the extra. She was concerned with his well being."

"Yes, of course. How much?"

"Ten dollars a session; two sessions; twenty dollars."

"That's fine. I will definitely be there tomorrow evening. Seven at the latest. Will Arielle be there?"

"If she isn't, you can leave it with me. I'll be sure she gets it. May I have your phone number"

"Yes, of course."

CHAPTER TWO

It didn't take me long at the fitness club. I was starting out slow. I didn't want to be so sore that I'd give up. I wanted to just make it a regular part of my routine without expecting results to avoid disappointment. It was a three day rotation of machines, running and swimming. I switched to a pre-work time slot so I could go to the stable after work.

I was grateful for the refresher work I had done in law vocabulary and ethics. Things had changed in ten years but Charlotte, the exiting secretary, was informative and helpful. I'd have her guidance the rest of the week and then she'd be moving on to bigger and better things for herself.

I was actually surprised at the speed with which the confidence was surging back into my life. I did enjoy the multi-tasking of a busy office. I remembered the glow of satisfaction in a job well done. I don't think they realized I saw the transaction out of the corner of my eye, but Charlotte gave Braddock Hartman a thumbs up gesture after only two and a half days of orientation at the office. The smile on his face was an uplifting reward, and encouraged me to think I was going to make it on my own.

After work, I followed the directions to Phoenix stables with butterflies playing tag in my stomach. Would I be able to handle Hudson or would I have to tuck my tail in humiliation? I took refuge in the fact that I was doing well at my job. I hadn't thought that was possible just a month ago. I insisted to myself that I could regain my enthusiasm for riding.

I wasn't prepared for the barns to be yellow, trimmed in orange, with a bronze thunderbird painted on the side. I'd need sunglasses to come here, I mentally joked.

I was following another car down the long lane. There was a waif of a child looking out the back window with a scowl on her face. I thought she should be strapped in a seat belt. I could see her mother half turning to speak to the girl. The car swerved a bit each time she looked back.

"I hope Hudson isn't stabled close to her horse," I muttered.

It was a busy place. Despite the chill, three horses were being ridden in an outdoor arena. Huge outdoor lights attempted to hold the encroaching darkness at bay. In the sand arena, a teenage girl was lunging a big liver chestnut that I realized was CastleontheHudson. My eyes were full of him. He had a wide blaze down his face, and a white sock on his left front leg. He was big; at least seventeen hands; beautiful. I was terrified. Other horses were being led into the indoor arena but I was only vaguely aware of them. I had the sinking feeling I was going to embarrass myself.

The waif child was now a devil child standing with fists on hips, feet spread. "Why haven't you come? Hudson was upset. He doesn't care so much now. He's made new friends. But you scared him. I hope he kicks you."

"Cindy, stop that! That's rude!" The woman looked at me apologetically. "I'm so sorry. She's very opinionated."

I wanted to say it was okay, but nothing came out. I offered only a weak smile. My heart fluttered as I realized she was probably right. What kind of horse owner was I? I wondered how many disapproving looks I was getting. I feared looking around to actually see. I felt frozen in my spot. The sound of Hudson's hoofs thudding in the sand reverberated in my ears. I wanted to run away and was about to turn toward the car when I felt a presence come up behind me.

"Hello. Are you Jewel Fitzgerald?"

I swallowed and turned to face her. "Yes. I am so sorry for not coming before now. You must think me horrible."

"It's always hard starting over," she soothed.

I felt compassion flow from her. She stuck out her hand. "I'm Shelly Weston; stable manager. I'll bet Hudson will be glad to see you here at last."

"Hudson doesn't really know me. I've only seen him once before. He was Angel's way of getting rid of a horse not spirited enough for her and of getting me back in the saddle. I used to be quite a rider ten years ago. Now, I'm not so sure."

"Did you have a bad fall that made you quit riding?"

"Yes. Marriage."

"Ah, well, it'll come back to you I'm sure. Let's go meet your redeemer. When I told Arielle you'd be coming she thought she'd lunge him to calm him down for you."

"I don't think I'll ride. I really expect to humiliate myself the first time."

We were walking toward the sand arena.

"Arielle, here's Jewel."

"Whoa," Arielle called softly to Hudson. He didn't, and she stepped in front of him still crooning "Whoa," setting him on his haunches. I marveled at her fearlessness and remembered I was such once.

She turned to me. "Hello Jewel. You've got a great horse. He's awesome."

I smiled. "I'm glad you think so."

She took the lead from it's resting spot draped over the arena rails, slipped the cavesson from his head, snapped the lead onto his halter and handed it to me. I just looked at it with Hudson's heavy breathing blowing in my face. When I didn't reach for the lead, the smile disappeared from her face.

"I owe you money for lunging him," I stammered and fished in my jeans pocket.

"That's not necessary. I really enjoyed working with him."

"Arielle, this is Jewel's first time with Hudson. Why don't you tag along with her in case she has a problem. Show her where things are." She turned back to me. "A whole set of equipment and tack was delivered with him so you're all set. Arielle will stay here while you cool him out. He's had a good work out so he should be pretty mild for you. Then you can groom him. Why don't you come to my office after you're done, Jewel. I want to give you your copy of the contract and rules."

I nodded but wondered if she was going to tell me to take my horse elsewhere. I reluctantly took the lead and started walking around the arena with Hudson's breath on my neck. Shelly talked with Arielle before going back to her office.

Arielle called, "Let him walk beside you."

I stepped over to allow him room between me and the rail. It was hard work walking in the sand. The grit was filling my canvass shoes.

"Turn him and walk the other way with you on his other side," she called to me. "He doesn't like going to the right so he'll resist but make him do it."

She was right. He wanted to walk over me. He towered above my head. It was difficult to keep him from turning in behind me. Stiff armed, I tried to keep his head off my left and his hoofs off my heels.

When Arielle finally said she thought he was dry enough, we walked back to a grooming bay. She showed me where his tack and grooming tools were in our very own tack locker. I had to smile that Angel had even supplied a bag of apple wafers.

Hudson eagerly took the treat from my hand. The hoof pick, stiff brush and soft brush felt familiar in my hands. Smiling, I naturally asked him to pick up his feet for picking and was grateful he did it well. My calves ached from walking in the sand and my arms soon followed suit from the unaccustomed work of brushing my horse.

"My horse," I said out loud as the bristles loosened dust and dry sweat from his coat. I was suddenly aware of his horsy aroma and the background smells of hay and grain. "I'm sorry I neglected you, Hudson," I whispered. "I'll do better, you'll see." He nuzzled my pocket where I had put a good-bye treat.

Hay and grain awaited Hudson in his stall. I gave him a final pat and held out the treat. He ignored both as his nose dove into his feed pan. With a sigh, I turned from his rejection and went to Shelly's office. She was at her computer. Arielle was filing something.

"Jewel, Angel signed temporary contracts but we need you to sign them as the owner. Here's a list of the rules. You might want to read over them before signing. If you don't feel you can handle them, you will, of course, need to move Hudson. You'll be reimbursed the boarding fee that's been paid in advance if you choose to leave. I must say being paid a year in advance is unusual."

The list wasn't long: riding at your own risk, visitors riding only your horse, no alcohol, no smoking, consideration of horses being worked, respect toward other boarders. I silently wondered if the devil child had read that last rule.

"I don't see a problem," I said and reached for the pen to sign the contract. "I'm paid through next April, correct?"

"That's right. Now another matter. You seem fearful of riding. Perhaps it would behoove you to take a few refresher lessons on tamer mounts."

"I like that idea, but I really need to be careful with my money until I start collecting a regular paycheck. Getting set up has taken a good deal of my available funds."

"I'm sure it has but Arielle is willing to give you the lessons for free in exchange for the privilege of riding Hudson until you're ready to take over that task."

My jaw dropped. "Sounds like I'm getting the better part of the bargain."

"I think I am," said the teen. "I'll bet he's an awesome ride. Besides, I'll bet it doesn't take you long to recover your equestrian skill. You just keep grooming him and getting to know him. You'll be throwing a leg over him in no time."

There was a pause. Then with a twinkle in her eye, she continued. "However, if you've a mind to, and feel guilty enough, you could help clean a few stalls on the weekends."

I smiled back. I was liking this young woman more and more. "Sounds fair. How many stalls?"

"Including cleaning their water buckets. Hudson's and my two horses: Cherry Tart and Cavalier."

"It's a deal. What time should I be here?"

"Sevenish. After the stalls are cleaned, I'll give you a lesson. You can ride all week to practice, whenever the horses aren't in use otherwise."

Driving home, I couldn't believe the kindness of Shelly and Arielle. Things were going to work out just fine. I was sure of it. I put the list of rules and the contract into a file folder, marked it "CastleontheHudson", showered and crawled into bed with a smile on my face and in my heart.

I had made it through my first week of a new job. When I woke up on Saturday morning and looked in the mirror, I saw a smile reflected back at me. If this was life after divorce, why did I wait so long?

I dressed and headed for Phoenix stables. I was excited to do the safe barn work and a little apprehensive about getting on a horse again. As nice as Shelly and Arielle had been, I felt sure they'd pick a suitable mount.

My grooming/lunging sessions with Hudson were getting more comfortable. It would take a good bit of work to eradicate his right side resistance, but Arielle said she would work him to the right under saddle as well so he'd be loosening up faster and would soon have no difficulty with it.

I paused in my chores to peek into the arena where Arielle was riding my horse and felt a surge of jealousy. She was a natural. She looked like she was part of him. She was asking him to do things that made my head spin; half passes, extended trots, collected canters, flying lead changes, circles, serpentines and figure eights. He was executing them beautifully.

When I finally went out for my lesson, I was disappointed to see an old mare with drooping head; saddled and waiting for me. Arielle saw the disappointed look on my face. She laughed as she handed me head phones and attached the radio pack to my waist band at the small of my back.

11

"Don't let Roxy fool you. She puts on the old nag show to help beginners get over their fear. Believe me, she'll size you up and give you a ride specifically geared to your capabilities."

I had my doubts. I mounted with comparative ease. I was even more pleased that my body automatically found the ear, shoulder, hip, heel alignment. Roxy's ears flicked.

"Go ahead and move out at a walk. Go around the arena to the right twice, then cut through the middle in a figure eight to go to the left."

I took up the reins and squeezed my calves against Roxy's sides. She calmly stepped out. After a few strides I held firm on the reins but squeezed her sides again and she picked up the tempo of her steps without breaking stride. I closed my eyes and felt my body move in sync with hers: felt her mouth on the bit. When I opened my eyes I glanced down and noticed my toes were turned out. I turned the whole lower legs inward at the knees. I was feeling the strain on my thighs. Arielle's voice in my ear calmly said to trot the same pattern.

I cued Roxy and she slid smoothly into her trot and I into posting. By the time we crossed through the center to reverse our direction, I was breathing hard and my thighs were screaming. I knew I'd be walking funny in the office on Monday.

"Walk," I heard Arielle command, and I gratefully slowed Roxy by stilling my seat. "Relax a bit," she added.

I let the reins slide through my fingers and Roxy stretched her neck, lowering her head to just above the sand floor of the arena. As we neared the far end of the arena, and I was shortening the reins again to bring Roxy's head back up, Arielle said to trot half an arena length and then go into a canter. I was pleased with how everything was coming back to me, but the command to canter made my heart skip. Tighten inside rein, outside heel to horse behind girth. Don't forget to breath. Roxy flowed from one pace into the next without missing a beat. We circled the arena once and permission was given to walk again.

"That was great Jewel."

"Thanks." I couldn't help but smile in satisfaction.

"When you practice this week, I want you to use Deek. Don't panic. He's a good schooling horse also. Roxy's an old girl. Can't take too much of the fancy or fast. You're way beyond needing her. Deek's capable too. He just won't give it without you asking politely. After watching you ride, I'm sure you'll have no trouble."

"I'll trust your judgment," I said a bit dubiously.

"After you cool Roxy and put her in stall 34, check out Deek in 35."

I gave Roxy a final pat as she stepped into her stall. She dropped her head to nibble the hay in the corner. I hooked the stall guard then stepped to the next stall to look over Deek, my practice mount for the next week. He was tall and black. He raised his head to look at me and dropped it back to his hay.

"Are you really harmless?" I asked him.

"He is indeed," said a male voice. "Hi. I'm Joe. I work here."

I shook his proffered hand. "I'm Jewel Fitzgerald. My friends call me Jules."

"Well, I sure hope we become friends, Jules."

"Do you have a horse here? Seems everybody that works here does."

"I show one of the Phoenix horses in three day eventing. Are you going to show?"

"I don't know if I'll have time."

"Arielle seems to think Hudson is really talented. It would be a shame to not utilize such talent. Are you coming to the Spring trail ride?"

"I'm not sure Hudson is much of a trail horse."

"Well, you've got until June to whip him into shape."

Joe's smile was dazzling, his blue eyes direct, his voice deeply masculine; thin waist and narrow shoulders. I knew he was a lot younger than me but I couldn't help the flutter in my stomach.

"Well, I need to go," I stammered.

"See you tomorrow?"

"Sure."

After lunch I went to the fitness center to work out. By then I was tired so I took a nap. I spent the evening reading. The dirty dishes still sat in the sink and I just smiled at them. Josh would be yelling at me if I were still married. On my own, I could be a slob if I wanted to be.

I had them washed before leaving for Phoenix stables the next morning. I knew I wasn't a slob. It was just nice to do things on my own terms. What a relief not to have to worry about pleasing anyone other than myself.

I groomed, tacked and lunged Hudson. Arielle took him over then. As I cleaned the three stalls, scrubbed the water buckets and feed pans I could hear his thudding hoof beats on the arena sand and dreamed of the day that would be me on his back. Then I tacked up Deek. Deek was a gentleman. He stood for mounting, his gaits were smooth, he gave what I asked for. We moved…well, almost as one. My whole body ached from the unaccustomed workouts at the fitness center and from the previous day's lesson on Roxy. I knew it was the price of inactivity for so long. I knew I was soon going to want to skip a day of exercise. I knew I must not give in to that temptation.

I was having a hard time keeping my eyes off Hudson. He knew so much. I couldn't believe he had that right side weakness or that Angel let him go for so much less than what most of her horses cost. "Just helping me," I reasoned.

I saw Joe leaning against the door frame of the arena. Arielle rode Hudson over to him, chatted and leaned down to kiss him. He turned his face away. She sat back up with a confused look on her face. He smiled and said something but Arielle had turned Hudson back into the arena, her face like stone.

As I came down the long side, I glanced at Joe still leaning at the same place. He was watching me. I didn't like what was happening. Were he and Arielle in a relationship? I couldn't believe my presence was creating a problem. He was so much younger than I. No matter what Joe's interest, I was not going to betray Arielle. She had been friendly and helpful. I truly wanted her as a friend, even though she was much younger than I was also. I owed her and I wasn't going to repay her by stealing her boyfriend.

14

The next thing I knew I was on my back in the sand of the arena. I'd lost the reins but Deek stood over me, waiting, looking at me as if asking, "Well?"

I heard Joe's booming laughter. Arielle was soon there and dismounted from Hudson.

"Are you alright?"

"Yes. Just stunned. What happened?"

"Did your mind wander?"

I sat up. "Afraid so."

"Deek expects all your attention to remain on him."

"Just like a man," I said as I picked myself up and brushed away the sand.

Arielle and I looked at each other and then we began to giggle.

CHAPTER THREE

Braddock Hartman was a busy man. He was one of only four lawyers in town. The other establishment was Stahlman, Stidd and Austin where they covered the whole range of legal services. Brad, however, limited himself to real estate, inheritances, wills and trusts. He took the unpleasant domestic issues of divorce and custody cases only when the monetary flow was low, which wasn't often.

Brad had a reasonable wife, Sara, who didn't squander his money and he loved her dearly. Charlotte had warned, only half jokingly, that to let him forget her birthday or their wedding anniversary was grounds for dismissal. Both days were marked with big red stickers on the calendar and she instructed that the first thing I was to do with a new calendar each year, before it was put into use, was to mark those special days.

Brad also gave me his kids' schedules so, if possible, I could keep him free to attend their functions. He had son and daughter twins in college in Damascus. Marcus played football and Mariah was in drama. He had a teen daughter, Heather, in high school and the youngest, Brooke, was in sixth grade. It wasn't long before I met them as they often popped in just to say "Hi" or to bring us a gift of cinnamon buns.

To enable Brad to get to games and drama productions, we worked through lunch and quit early on Fridays. He even got me tickets so I could go. It seemed I was almost one of the family.

Of course, that meant we worked longer on other days; usually Wednesdays. I didn't mind starting early and staying late one day a week to have a short day on Friday. Mondays we usually worked through lunch but didn't leave early. He brought finger sandwiches, veggie trays and even sweets made up by Sara so we didn't go hungry.

It was one of those late hour Wednesdays when Mrs. Souder came in. She had on too much makeup and her heels were at least four inches. She seemed nervous. I let Brad know she was there. His first sight of her caused a flicker of confusion to cross his face as if he were trying to remember where he'd seen her before. They emerged from his office twenty minutes later, both with tension-stretched faces.

"I'll be in touch," she said.

Brad replied nothing as he watched her leave. Then to me he said, "Jewel, call Greg Rafferty. Put him through to my office."

"Yes, sir."

Greg was a private investigator Brad used occasionally. Usually he just told me what he needed Greg to check out, but this case seemed to be a private matter.

Wednesday was the one day of the week I didn't go to the stables because we worked late. I usually rented a movie or curled up with a book after work. Occasionally I'd sit on my balcony and watch people on the street below. I was preparing a salad, this Wednesday, when the phone rang.

"Hey, this is Joe. How about grabbing a bite to eat with me?"

"Sorry Joe, I just made a salad."

"Refrigerate it. It'll be okay to eat tomorrow."

"I don't think so. I just got off work. This is my downtime night."

"Come on."

"Look Joe, aren't you with Arielle?"

"Was. Time to move on."

"Have you told her?"

"She's a smart cookie. She'll get the message."

Rae D'Arcy

"That's kind of insensitive. Don't think I want to date a guy that will just expect me to 'get the message' when he's ready to move on."

"You're different."

"How would you know? You've only just met me."

"You're older. I'll bet you aren't clingy. You can stand on your own."

"Arielle doesn't strike me as clingy. And speaking of age, I'm sure I'm too old for you."

"You know what they say about older women."

I felt my ire rise. "No, I don't know and let me rephrase, you're too young for me."

I really wanted to say 'too immature' but thought I needn't be that cruel yet. I could hope he'd get the message.

"Are you coming to the Spring trail ride?"

"I was thinking about it."

"You should. It's fun."

"I'll see how Hudson does out on the trail before I decide."

"So when are you going to start riding him?"

"Soon."

Fact of the matter was, I thought as I ate my salad, I was getting excited about riding Hudson. I had visualized it in my mind often. He seemed manageable under Arielle's tutelage. My confidence had grown as I went from horse to horse on my lessons and practice riding. The memory of balance and cues flooded my mind and body. The feel of a responsive horse beneath me revived the thrill of equine power at my finger tips.

From Deek, I had progressed to Argo, Cherry Tart and even Cavalier, although I had the feeling that riding Arielle's horses were to help exercise them while she was working with CastleontheHudson. I gratefully considered it a fair trade. As the soreness from my work-outs at the fitness club and from riding began to fade, and I felt new firmness in my body, I was sure it was time to claim my horse.

Thursday Brad still seemed tense.

"Jewel, reschedule our Tuesday morning appointments for any available times, and if Mrs. Souder should call, schedule her no sooner than the following week."

"Yes sir."

That evening at the stables, Hudson seemed eager. His ears were pricked. He kept nuzzling me as I tried to get him groomed and tacked. I wondered what had him so worked up. Maybe this was the wrong time to try to ride him.

"It's about time," said the devil child I'd tried so hard to avoid since starting to come to the stables.

"Excuse me?"

She had her fists perched at her waist on non-existent hips but she had a smile on her face. "He says it's about time you rode him. He likes your hands. They're gentle when you groom him. He's sure you'll be easy on his mouth."

"You know what he's thinking?"

"Sure. Have a good ride."

There was a woman standing a few feet behind Cindy. She was grinning also and approached as the child went to get her own horse. "Hi. I'm Madison Kurt, owner of Phoenix Stables."

"Hello. I've heard a lot about you."

"Sorry it has taken me so long to get down here to meet you. By the way, Cindy is our resident animal communicator. If she says Hudson is excited about you finally riding him, you can be sure he is."

I felt a thrill that my horse was looking forward to me getting on his back, but also a bit anxious at his exuberance.

"You look scared and excited," Madison continued.

I laughed. "You're very perceptive."

"So this will be your first time astride?"

"Yes."

"I'll stay in the arena to keep an eye on you. I don't know if you noticed but there is always someone in the judge's box. They're sort of like a life guard. So even if I'm not around, someone is."

"Wow. That's a great idea and very reassuring. Well, here goes."

I led Hudson to the mounting block in the near corner of the arena. He stood in one place but couldn't help pawing in his excitement. I refused to mount until he quit, as I had seen Arielle do. It took an effort to breathe deep to calm myself. I waited an instant more, then squeezed my calves against Hudson's barrel and felt him flow into a walk.

There was no other way to describe him other than fluid. I kept him in the walk for sometime although I could feel the energy gathering in the powerful body beneath me. I finally cued him for a trot, and like water whose pathway narrows, he changed his gait and picked up speed without a jolt. He extended and collected on command. I could see us as from a distance in my mind's eye as our bodies communicated, and we looked good.

I was beginning to sweat but Hudson was breezing. I asked for a canter and felt like I was on a magic carpet ride. I could feel my face split into a grin. I asked Hudson to slow and he dropped smoothly into a trot, and then a walk.

I saw Madison was smiling as I walked Hudson toward her.

"Jewel, you both looked like you were having the time of your life."

Between pants, I agreed.

"It would be a shame if you didn't show."

"Well, we'll see. It was awesome, but I think I've got a lot to accomplish before I go out in public."

"Not as much as you think. Arielle says he's great at dressage. She could get you ready to show."

"I'll talk to her about it."

"Are you coming to the June trail ride? I hear you're new to the area. It's a great way to meet people."

"I'll have to see how Hudson does out on the trail."

"Well, enjoy yourself until I tack up Fritz and then we'll take them out and see how he does."

"Alright. Thanks for your help."

CHAPTER FOUR

Even though it began to rain, nothing could dampen my happiness. I was happy at work, happy at Phoenix, happy in my colorful apartment. I was typing up wills, researching deeds and titles, and hearing the stories behind it all. I was riding my fabulous horse and paying Arielle for dressage lessons. I was also helping her with her barn chores just because I liked her and enjoyed being at the barn. Arielle and her friend Darla occasionally popped in at my apartment to watch chick flicks and eat pizza. But even if I was alone, I felt safe, at peace, and good about where and what I was.

We never discussed Joe. Arielle did, indeed, get the message and managed to treat him respectfully as if they had never been a couple but always friends. I gave him no encouragement and his amour finally faded as he directed his interest toward another stable hand named Bonnie, who seemed more worldly wise and able to handle his game playing with a bit of her own.

It seemed nothing could go wrong, but of course that's the precise moment it will. It hadn't really struck me as unusual the first time the Wednesday veggie tray came from Jonell's deli in the local grocery. I guess I figured Mrs. Hartman was just too busy to make it herself. But all the Wednesday and Friday goodies seemed to be coming on a regular basis from Jonell's. Still it didn't click until Mrs. Souder walked into the office on a Friday just before we were leaving.

Brad was commenting about Mariah playing the part of Repunzal in the production of Into the Woods, and Brooke's birthday was the same day. What to do? How to divide his time? Greg was picking at the leftover finger food I was bagging up for Brad to take home.

"Take Brooke to see the production, and then let her dress up for a meal in a fancy restaurant afterwards," I said just as she walked in.

"Brad, may I speak to you?"

Brad? They were on a first name basis? When did that happen? What was on her face? Contrition? Pleading? Sorrow?

He responded coldly. "Is it necessary?"

"It is to me."

Greg was still picking. He hadn't even turned to look at her. I saw his hand slip inside his jacket; heard the slight click of the tape recorder button he pushed on.

Mrs. Souder glanced at Greg and I and back to Brad. "In private."

"I think I should have a witness to anything you say to me."

"Brad, please understand...."

"Understand what?"

"Why I...why I...I had to do it for Courtney. I didn't involve you until I couldn't do it on my own anymore."

"Commendable of you. What did it get you?"

She hesitated and then barely above a whisper she said, "Nothing."

"But it sure got me something, didn't it?"

She dropped her eyes. "I'm sorry." She spun and quickly retreated with the soft tapping of her loafers seeming to put defeat in quotation marks and the loafers themselves seeming to be a statement of submission.

I put on my coat and handed the leftovers to Brad as I reached for the door knob.

He grasped my hand with the bag. "Aren't you going to ask what's going on?"

I looked directly into his brown eyes. "If you want me to know, I'm sure you'll tell me."

He smiled at me. "I appreciate that. Let's all go out for dinner. My treat."

"Sorry, I've got plans," refused Greg.

"And do you have a date?" he asked me.

My insides quivered. Normally there was no problem with eating dinner with the boss on a professional basis. But as my mind skipped from clue to clue like a flat rock over a smooth pond, I sensed this was a deeply personal matter and I didn't want to add to the foul smell of a stagnant pond.

"With my horse," I responded weakly.

"Ouch. I've lost out to a horse."

"He's a very fine looking horse."

"That's suppose to make me feel better?"

I grinned sheepishly.

"Very well. I'll see you on Monday."

When I got home from the stables, I was all aflutter with how well Hudson and I had done on our level one pattern. It was like I had memories of doing it before. It was more than déjà vu. My body remembered the patterns and cues, and I had to wonder again where they came from. Arielle had convinced me to try a show. I'd have to start in novice but we started practicing the level two patterns, just because after going through them a couple times, I remembered them and Hudson executed them with precision.

I just got in the door when the phone rang.

"Hello."

"Jules, what have you been up to?"

"Angel! How good to hear your voice. Every thing is going wonderfully. Thank you, thank you for your help in establishing me in my new life."

"How's CastleontheHudson.?"

"He is so awesome. We're going to our first dressage show in June. You must come and watch."

"Sounds kind of tame compared to what you used to do."

"Well, yes, but I'm really enjoying it. I might get into eventing some day, but right now Hudson and I are just enjoying each other. He knows so much more than I do."

"You used to tear over hedges and fences like you and the horse had wings."

I laughed nervously. "I just pointed the horse at the obstacle, gave him a kick and held on for dear life. Dressage takes control and team work."

"So now you're better than I am?"

"No Angel, no. I'm saying I love this horse you sold me. I am so indebted to you for helping me find myself again. Eventually, I might be less fearful, but I'm not there yet. Can you come for a visit?"

"Sounds like you're doing fine without me."

"Oh Angel, I owe you so much. How are things going with you?"

"Quite well. Got a group coming next weekend for a race. You should come. Let's see what sort of mettle your dressage horse has over a real course."

I heard the chill in her voice and it froze my heart. "Angel, that's a bit too close to Josh. And I'm really not that daring yet."

Her laugh was harsh. "I'll never forgive Josh for destroying you. See you around."

I stood holding the receiver to my ear long after the dial tone started. I finally hung up with a shaking hand.

I ran a tub of hot water, added some lavender scent to calm me and climbed in to soak. As the hot water steamed the tension out of my knotted muscles I remembered meeting Angel at a company party at my first job: Thompson, Thompson, Gregory and Blume. Angel was married to Blume. Her penchant for dangerous races was in response to the boring life she led, she had explained. Alexander Blume was an exceptional criminal lawyer but a stamp collector at home.

The memories flooded over me. Big boned horses, sweating, snorting as they charged over unkempt hedges, fences in ill repair, rocky drop offs, through rivers, sliding down escarpments on their haunches, sometimes returning to the barn bleeding. Some of the riders returned bleeding as well. At first it was scary and then exhilarating. Then I needed to face death in each ride to feel alive. Everything else was boring. The day Bill Tadaro came home under a white sheet, I knew I had to do something about my danger addiction. Despite the thrill of facing death, I wasn't ready to die.

Josh was controlling. With a shock I realized that was exactly why I married him. I needed someone to rein me in to keep me from killing myself. The tears ran down my cheeks as I realized how thankful I was to Josh for saving me; how sad I was that I used him; how scared I was to feel the pendulum swinging back the other way.

"Oh, please God, don't let it swing too far," I cried.

For a moment I wished Angel didn't know where I lived. Despite what I owed her, I didn't like the hold she had had on me. Would she pull me back into her world of thrills, rushing adrenaline, ripping flesh?

How cruel it had been to the horses. Why had I not thought of that? Why had I thought I needed thrills at that time? Where did I learn to ride with balance and soft hands? Certainly not on Angel's horses.

Monday was busy. Mrs. Souder called twice but Brad refused to take the calls. We were both tired by five.

"How about a drink to decompress?" asked Brad.

I grimaced. "Sorry. Going to the stables."

"Afterward?"

"Brad...."

"Jules, I need to tell you what's going on."

"Okay. I'll smell like horse but I'll meet you for a coffee afterwards."

I worried about the rendezvous on the drive to the stables. I was afraid it would affect my diligence in dressage practice, but once I was astride Hudson, all else was forgotten. In fact I was still feeling euphoric on the drive home and almost forgot to stop at the diner for that promised cup of coffee.

It was drizzling and the spring air had a chill. The air conditioning in the diner made me shiver. Sara, Heather and Brooke were sitting at a table. Sara looked tired. Brooke was pouting, and Heather seemed to be mothering them both.

"Hello, Sara. How are you?"

"Hello Jules."

"You look tired. I hope everything is okay."

"She IS tired," snapped Brooke.

Heather grinned. "She's tired of Brooke being hormonal."

"Aren't you a bit young to be hormonal," I joked to Brooke.

Heather broke in again. "She's competing with Mariah in drama."

I kept my eyes on Brooke. "I guess we all have drama in our lives." I turned to Sara. "If there's anything I can do, let me know. I could take Heather and Brooke to a movie to give you some down time."

"That's kind of you Jules."

"Ulterior motives. I much prefer your food to Jonell's."

Sara's eye brows dropped and two crease lines appeared between them. Her lips went thin. I sensed it was time to retreat. "Well, I'll leave you ladies to yourselves. The offer stands Sara. Just let me know."

I made my way to a table in a corner and wondered why Brad would arrange to meet me without saying his family would be there as well? Unless he didn't realize his family would be there. Why was she tired? Why was she angry?

The bell over the door jangled and Brad walked in. He saw them immediately and went straight to them. Brooke's face broke into a smile. She jumped up and hugged him. Heather smiled but kept her seat. He was talking to Sara who scowled and repeatedly shook her head. Finally, she stood, grabbed her jacket and purse. Brad tried to pick up the tab but Sara snatched it from his hand.

"I don't want to go," yelled Brooke.

Brad said something to her.

"NO."

Sara gave the tab and money to Heather to pay, grabbed Brooke by her arm and dragged the child screaming like a three year old out the door. Heather came back to give her father a kiss and to say "I love you," before she too left.

Brad stood looking after them, his shoulders slumped, his face gone slack with sadness. The other diners who had been watching the scene went back to the business of their meals and the waitresses stopped gawking, grabbed coffee pots and circulated with refills. One of them, Becky, touched Brad's arm, asking if he wanted something. He smiled at her, shook his head 'no' and left.

I was in shock. What had happened to that close knit happy family? Whatever it was, I was sure it had to do with Mrs. Souder.

I was already at my desk when Brad walked in the next morning. His face looked tired and I wondered if he had gotten any sleep. As soon as he saw me, realization hit him.

"Oh Jules, I totally forgot last night."

"It's alright. I was there. I'll get us some coffee and you can tell me what you need to."

Brad sat with his hands around the ceramic cup that Charlotte had gotten him as if trying to warm his self. It said "Best Boss."

"In my first year of college, I had a one night stand with a Kim Bailey," he began. "It was my first sexual encounter. I wasn't very good, but she was. I was enthralled with her. She didn't want to continue the relationship after that. I called her a few times but finally let it go. Never heard from her again. I found other relationships and interests. Kim Bailey met and quickly married Ervin Souder, a business major with dreams of starting his own business. According to Kim, he tried several and all of them folded. He committed suicide several years ago. Kim has been raising her daughter on her own since then. Not doing too badly. Now it's college time and she felt she needed help. She was pretty sure the girl was mine, so she tracked me down. The week before I told you to schedule a follow up appointment with her was spent taking a paternity test and telling Sara about the positive result.

"I didn't meet Sara until my senior year of college. She was an accountant major. I'm not sure why Sara is so upset. She wasn't a virgin either. I would have helped Kim if I'd known I had a daughter. I'm debating whether to still help with college expenses, even though

27

the court ruled in my favor because Kim waited so long to include me in Courtney's life. And she perjured herself on the stand. She said she called me and told me about the baby, but we got phone records and there were no calls from her to me after that night. Kim got nothing but court costs. I lost my family over an indiscretion that happened before I met Sara. I think Kim thinks, if Sara leaves me, I'll take her."

"Would you?"

"No."

"Is divorce in the works?"

"Not yet. Sara took the kids and moved to her mom's. She's a CPA. Maybe she's trying to see if she can make it on her own."

"Then you haven't lost them yet. Have you any interest in Courtney?"

"My gosh, I didn't know she existed until a month ago. I feel some obligation for financial assistance. The thought has crossed my mind to get to know her, but I think that would drive Sara away faster and maybe give false hope to Kim. What do you think?"

"I think you should do what you know is right and let the chips fall where they will."

CHAPTER FIVE

It was show day. Half the boarders at Phoenix were show people. Several of the workers and riding students would be competing as well. We were all at the stables by four o'clock in the morning loading foot lockers; applying shipping wraps to the legs of glossy-hide horses.

Hudson and I were hitching a ride with Roger McManus and his wife Sherry. She was showing a big Hanoverian named Special Package. Pack and Hudson were pasture mates and got along well. We would also both be returning at the end of the day, while others remained to compete on Sunday.

Darla was riding Cherry Tart in level three dressage. Lori on Parcheesi, Arielle on Jumping Jack Flash, Joe on Boudoir, Josie on Here He Comes, and Alyssa on Amazing Girl, were all competing in three day eventing and had been at the show grounds since Friday afternoon. Arielle was also showing Cavalier in arena Jumping.

Novice class dressage was the first event on Saturday. I ignored the crowd, focused on me and Hudson, and left with a first place ribbon. That was it. I knew I was hooked.

Roger was baby sitting the horses so Sherry and I could mingle with the other horse folk. As I wandered through the crowd, I saw Sara and Brooke in the stands.

"Hey," I called as I made my way to them.

"I love your horse, Jules," gushed Brooke.

"Thanks, I'm pretty partial to him myself. What brings you to the show? Do you know someone competing?"

"No. Brooke likes to come and watch."

"Can I ride your horse, Jules?"

"Do you know how to ride?"

Her face fell. "No. Could you teach me?"

"I'm not sure how I'd be as a teacher, but they give lessons where I board Hudson."

"Oh, mom, could I?"

"We'll see how much they cost. And you'll have to figure out how you'd get there and home again."

Heather will be driving soon. She can take me."

"She needs a car first, sweety."

Brooke crossed her arms, scowled and threw herself onto the seat. "You never let me do anything fun."

I laughed, trying to ease the tension. "Walking all the way to the stables sure wouldn't be fun. Sara, do you mind if I take Brooke for a ride? I'll lead so there's no danger of him running off with her."

"I was thinking of going to get something to eat."

"Well, let's all go. I'm feeling a bit hungry myself. Then I'll take Brooke for a ride and bring her safely back to you…unless you'd like to go for a ride also."

Sara smiled. "No, I'd rather come back here to watch the competition."

"Okay. Let's eat."

I was leading Hudson out among the cars parked in the field with Brooke on his bare back. I finally stopped to let him drop his head to graze.

"So, Brooke, if you love horses how come you don't have one?"

"Mom says because I'll just grow up, go away to college, and they'll be stuck with it."

"Your parents are going through a hard time right now."

"It's Mom's fault. Why get upset over something that happened before they even met."

"Maybe your mom just thought she was his only love, I don't know. Maybe it's just the shock of it. How do you feel about having a half sister?"

"I HATE her for breaking up my family!"

"She didn't do it, Brooke. Her mom just wanted help sending her to college."

"Do you think Dad should have to pay for her college?"

"That isn't for me to say. I'm just trying to see her mom's point of view. No one wants their children to suffer from lack of education. Life is so much harder without it."

"That isn't my fault."

"No, it isn't. Nor is it Courtney's, or your parents' fault either."

"Why couldn't she just get school loans?"

"That would have been the logical thing to do. Come on, I'll show you how to groom."

I was crawling into bed that night before I realized I hadn't seen Angel at the show. Disappointment and relief swirled around me like oil and water being stirred in the same container. Angel had done so much for me and yet...and yet....

Monday evening I saw Madison at the stables taking Fritz over some jumps. Hudson and I were working over smaller ones. As soon as I saw her cooling her mount, I rode next to her.

"Madison, I know a young girl who would like to learn to ride. I know you have a work/ride program. There might be transportation problems as well. Have you any ideas?"

"Well, why don't you mentor her?"

"I'm not sure of my teaching skills."

"We have the instructors. You'll need to arrange her days to be here to work and see that she gets here and home again. You'll have to check the schedule in the lounge to see which days need workers and when the beginner horses are available. Make sure she gets with whatever stable hand is available at that time. Shelly will help you arrange everything. See if you can come at those same times so you can provide transportation."

"What if she can pay?"

"We still insist they groom the lesson mount."

"Okay, I'll check it out."

I had soup heating to offset the damp chill of another rainy, spring evening as I made the phone call to Sara. "Sara, it's Jules. Hey, I'm not trying to cause trouble but they have a work-for-lessons program at the stables where I board my horse."

"Payment isn't really the issue Jules. I don't think she wants the responsibility. She just wants the fun part of riding."

"Ah, I see. Well, if she's interested, they do insist they groom their lesson horse. That might give her a taste of the work part. I can take her out with me and transport her back home."

"Jules, that's out of your way."

"It'll only be once a week...unless she wants to work for extra riding time. I'd really like to give her the chance. They have a lesson opening on Tuesday evening. I know that's a school night."

"Brooke's a pretty good student. I doubt one night will hurt. School will soon be out for summer break. Maybe it will do her some good."

"You'll need to go out to sign Risk and Payment contracts. Can you arrange that?"

"I'll go out the night of her first lesson. Is that alright?"

"I think so."

Tuesday evening Sara brought Brooke to Phoenix stables. She signed the necessary forms and turned the child over to the instructor. I walked her back to her car.

"Sara, it's none of my business, but why are Kim and Courtney an issue?"

She smiled thinly. "Not an issue. Just an excuse."

"You were already thinking of leaving? You seemed so happy. I know Brad doesn't want to lose you."

"He doesn't want me to have any independence, would be a better description."

"But he seems so attentive."

"Controlling is more the word. I make his life run smoothly. If I had any activities of my own that caused bumps in his life, it would be an entirely different matter."

My face flushed as I realized I should be supporting Sara, as I had so recently escaped from just such a trap. "Sara, I'm sorry I stuck my nose in where it didn't belong. I was getting only one side of the story. Please, if there is anything I can do to help you, let me."

She smiled. "Bringing Brooke here each Tuesday evening to give me a few hours to myself will be an immense help."

"You got it."

My life was settling into a comfortable rhythm. The spring was exceptionally cool and wet. There were, however, a few sunny dry days that inspired people to get out, whether to walk the path in the town park or ride the horses out on the trail at Phoenix stables. Hudson had lots of company to help him become a good trail horse and I met many of the other boarders there.

The cooler temperatures made dressage classes more pleasant, but the rain created a risky outdoor jump course. You could tell which riders had confidence in their mounts and which mounts had nervous riders. Those horses lost faith and balked at jumps they were capable of clearing. I envied Arielle and Lori their calm and style. Their horses performed wonderfully even in the pouring rain. By next year, I promised myself, I would be competing in show jumping as well as dressage.

Brooke turned out to be a bit of a complainer. I could see why Sara was appreciating a few hours without her. It didn't take long for me to lose my enthusiasm for transporting her to Phoenix on Tuesday evenings. Sara had also been right about Brooke not liking the work of grooming her mount, and she complained about the lessons at the walk being boring. I was going to give it at least six weeks and then suggest she quit if she didn't like it. I knew I'd be letting Sara down, but I just wasn't selfless enough to suffer through anymore of Brooke's whining. I was relieved that I only had to deal with it one night a week to and from Phoenix. Once we got to the stable, the instructor took her in hand and I could enjoy myself with Hudson.

The stable was abuzz with talk of the trail ride. I was hoping Brooke wasn't going to ask to go along. I was ashamed that I wasn't a very good mentor. I had just put Hudson back in his stall with his feed. The evening sky had donned its robe of dusk. As I was leaning against the car, I could see Brooke coming from the other wing. She was stomping and had a scowl on her face. On a trajectory to intercept her was Cindy who was also scowling and stomping.

"Roxy doesn't like you," she screamed.

Brooke stopped in her tracks and glared at the waif child. I saw two heads peer around door frames to watch the encounter.

"So what," Brooke hissed. "I don't like her either. She's dirty."

"That's because you don't groom her good enough."

"Why don't you groom her before I get here if you don't like it?" Brooke spun on her heels and ran toward the car.

"That's your responsibility," shouted Cindy to the retreating back.

I waited until we were down the lane and turning onto the main road heading for Montaine before I asked, "What's wrong?" to the hunched form hiding behind crossed arms.

"Did you hear that brat?"

I bit the inside of my cheeks at who was calling who a brat. "It looked like you were already mad when you came out of the stables."

"I asked Josie about the trail ride. She said I couldn't come because I couldn't ride good enough."

"That would be for your own safety."

"Stupid horse."

"Why stupid horse?" I asked remembering Roxy's ability to size up a rider.

"She bucked me off. That's why the stupid instructor thinks I can't ride. She doesn't let me do anything except walk. It was the stupid horse's fault."

"Brooke, you have to learn proper balance before you can trot. In fact, if you had balance, maybe you could have kept your seat."

"I'm not going back."

"Don't give up. Try harder." I said it but didn't mean it. I could feel my face reddening with the lie.

"Josie said I wasn't allowed to come back until I could control my temper. I'll show her. I'll make Dad get me my own horse."

Sara greeted her petulant child with a smile. "How was your lesson, sweety?"

"Fine," lied Brooke as she stomped to her room slamming the door behind her.

"I guess tonight was her last night, Sara."

"I know. Shelly called and explained."

"I guess you told me so, huh?"

"It's alright Jules. You tried."

"Maybe I can still come break you now and again?"

"You're a brave soul. I think I'll insist Brad take her once a week. That will work."

CHAPTER SIX

The last days of spring were hot and dry. The mud puddles dried up, cracked to look like jigsaw puzzles and by the night of the trail ride had been pulverized back into dust by horse and human traffic. The night of the trail ride, however, was humid.

As dusk arrived, horses and people streamed in from afar. Snap shirts, bolos and cowboy boots faced off with riding breeches, paddock boots and half chaps. Shelly, Madison, Arielle, Josie and other stable hands were collecting fees and checking shot records. I couldn't believe the crowd. I looked for a familiar face and found one.

"Hi, Sherry. Where's Roger?"

"He came out earlier to help transport the food out to the bonfire site."

"There sure are a lot of people here."

"Yep. The Phoenix trail rides are a big to do around here. People come from several states away. It just grows every year. They have to RSVP so I'll bet one of these days they'll have to turn people away. I'd recommend you get Hudson tacked. Pretty soon people will be wanting to pair up and talk. You'll want to be ready to go."

The heat and humidity caused a sheen of moisture on my brow and under my thin cotton, long sleeved shirt by the time I had Hudson ready to go. Most of the young riders had short sleeved T-shirts on. The pissst of the aerosol cans of mosquito guard were sounding all around, but the smell of Wipe and Endure were more prominent. The sprays for humans never worked very well for me. I chose long sleeves instead, and that didn't always protect me either. I was praying for a breeze when a tall sandy-haired man approached.

"Hi. I'm Jeremiah Johnson. You're new here aren't you?"

"Yes. I moved to Montaine in March. I'm Jewel Fitzgerald.

Precious or semi-precious?" He grinned at his own joke.

I laughed but didn't answer.

"I've never missed one of Madison's trail rides. They're great gatherings. She'll be instructing us to pair up with someone we don't know, and I know most everybody. Do you mind if I ride with you?"

"That's fine, I guess."

Hudson was already damp from the humidity. His head was high, eyes bright and ears pricked at all the new horses. His aroma hung in the moist atmosphere. I breathed him in deeply and felt gratitude at having him. I sent a silent 'thank you' to Angel for finding him deficient and selling him to me. The multitude of human voices blended together to sound like the hum of a bee hive. The smell of leather filled our nostrils, and pest repellants hung heavy in the air. The excitement and expectation was palpable. At last the call to "Mount up" rang through the air.

"May I give you a leg up?" asked Jeremiah before I could even look for a mounting block.

"Sure. Thanks."

We were moving into the double line when I noticed a woman staring intently at me. I thought she and her partner fell in behind us, but I didn't want to turn to look. It was unsettling, and I felt her eyes boring into my back.

Jeremiah chatted on. "Where are you originally from?"

"Not here."

"Ha. Secretive. Are you in the witness program?"

"No. Just don't want to be surprised by ghosts from the past showing up."

"I see."

37

"So, what do you do?" I asked trying to turn the topic away from me.

"I'm a newspaper editor."

"That must be fun. How long have you been doing that?"

"About ten years now at the Junction Herald. I'm thinking it's about time to move on."

"Why?"

"I like change and challenge. I joined the Herald when it was on the verge of going under. It's strong now. I need to find another weakling to build up."

"Does your wife want to move?"

He smiled. "Not married. Haven't found that special one yet. Thought I had, but I can't seem to get her to feel the same about me."

"That's a shame."

"Yes, it is. Are you married?"

"Recently divorced. Not ready for another relationship yet."

"Sounds wise. Safety in numbers."

"I'm not interested in numbers either. Just trying to rediscover myself."

"What do you do?"

"I work for an attorney."

"Para legal?"

"Executive secretary."

"Like it?"

"I do. The multitasking, hectic pace, constant prioritizing. It's quite a challenge. So, if you had a wife, would she want to move?"

"I'm afraid she wouldn't have a choice."

"But what if she worked a job she liked and didn't want to leave?"

"She wouldn't have a choice."

My spine stiffened at his answer and Hudson skipped sideways.

Jeremiah chatted on and made me feel he was interested in me as a person and wasn't just putting on the moves. He asked about books I had read and if I cared that poor Pluto had been demoted from planet status to giant fart. We discussed movies and taking God out of the pledge of allegiance. There was no argumentativeness, just interest in what I felt about those issues. It all made me want to feel comfortable with him, but his "no choice" comment wouldn't let me.

The horses were picking up the pace. The bonfire was crackling ahead and casting its guiding light as far as the newly leafed branches would allow it.

"Thank you for the pleasure of your company, Jewel. Enjoy yourself."

We loosened girths, removed bridles, and tied our horses to the hitching line. I turned to join the growing crowd around the tables, but felt a soft touch on my arm.

"Jewel? Jewel Fitzgerald?"

"Yes?" I looked at the woman who had scrutinized me earlier. Her face was kindly, though reaching toward elderly. I searched my brain for a memory.

"You don't remember me?"

"No. Should I?"

"I'm Gloria Simmons. I was your case manager."

My mind started buzzing. I couldn't respond.

"I'm sorry Jewel. I can see I've upset you. I didn't mean to ruin your evening. Are you all right?"

"I'm s-s-sorry. I don't remember…I feel I should but…."

"Did they not ever take you for counseling?"

"Who?"

"Your foster parents."

"Foster parents?"

"After what your father had done, we thought it was imperative you have counseling. Money was provided for the Meleskys to do just that."

Unnamed faces popped in and out of my mind. Who did these images belong to? Darkness played at the edges of my vision.

"When?" was all I could whisper.

"You were twelve. I'm so sorry Jewel. You've obviously blocked it out. I didn't mean to upset you. Please forgive me."

She hurried away leaving me standing in the dark. Although a chill had come over me, I backed away from the beckoning firelight until I felt the warmth of a horse to lean against. My head felt like it would explode. My lungs were burning and then I realized I needed to take a breath. The first inhale of air, heavy with moisture, didn't help much. I was seeing stars. I turned and grabbed a handful of mane to hold me upright. The horse turned his head and nuzzled my hip. It was Hudson. It was like he was saying he was here to support me and it would be all right. I felt a breeze on the back of my neck. I turned to breath in the next one. I felt better.

"Thanks Hudson," I whispered.

"Party is over here," called a dark form coming from between the trees.

"I'm coming."

"Are you okay?"

"I think so."

"I'm Marshall Provost. Gloria said she stirred up a hornets nest and thought her continued presence would only exacerbate it. She was very concerned and asked me to go check on you."

"I'm okay now."

"She really feels bad about whatever happened."

"Please, assure her I'll be fine."

I tried to smile but couldn't get my lips to cooperate, and it wasn't as easy as I had hoped to put it aside. What had I blocked out? Why all of a sudden did I feel uncomfortable in this large mix of people? I filled my plate with food and tried to circulate among the women. A few men asked me to dance, and although I was smiling at those on the dance floor and my feet wanted to tap time, I always said no because my plate was full. So I had to keep it full to be able to use that excuse.

I couldn't help notice how Jeremiah circulated. No one was left out of his field of attention. I saw him dance with a ten year old and felt an involuntary shudder. He spoke with matrons and pulled wall flowers from the sidelines. He even asked me to dance but I said I wasn't in a dancing mood. He simply touched my cheek and said, "Set it aside long enough to have a good time."

How could someone so sensitive be so insensitive, I marveled?

The air was cooling and felt good. The dancers were still sweating, however. I was especially enjoying watching the enthusiastic youngsters, some of whom were from the saddle club which used the Phoenix stable facility. The saddle club was started by Clint Flowers, a recently retired veterinarian. Madison now owned Montaine's only veterinarian clinic, and she still worked there part time. I wondered at her energy level, which enabled her to juggle her veterinarian responsibilities as well as run Phoenix and oversee the saddle club.

Marshall appeared in a chair next to mine. "You aren't dancing."

"I've eaten too much. The food was absolutely outstanding."

"So the trick is to not let you eat, if a guy wants you to dance?"

I couldn't help but smile. "No. I think I'm just not in the mood tonight."

"I sure hope you're in the mood at the fall trail ride," he smiled. "You disappointed an awful lot of men tonight. Not good for the image of Madison's trail rides." He smiled. "I don't ride but I could be sure a woman partners with you for the trip back to the barn if that will help."

"Thanks. That's very considerate of you."

CHAPTER SEVEN

The nightmares started. Sometimes they were groping hands and drool on featureless faces. Other times, I'd awake terrified that someone was in my apartment. I was fine at work where the pace kept my mind occupied. I was fine at the stables were Hudson's presence corralled my awareness. I was even fine at home, until it was time to sleep. My ghosts waited in the dreamscape to harass me.

I was showing almost every weekend and racking up points. I started schooling over jumps at Phoenix, and hoped to be showing in arena jumping before the show season was over.

I called Sara every few nights to see how she was doing. We arranged to go for ribs at Bubba's in Groveport on Sunday evening. Brad would have the kids. During the drive, it seemed we both visibly let our tension fly out the car windows.

As we took our seats and looked around the dim rustic interior, our eyes followed the muscle shirts and exposed biceps that flexed with sheens of moisture in the warm interior. Cowboy and work boots thumped to the lively country song. T-shirts and tight jeans coursed the narrow spaces between the tables.

I asked, "So how's it going?"

"Good. My therapist thinks I might be strong enough to reconcile with Brad and hold my ground about not letting him control me."

"Have you talked to Brad about getting back together?"

The boot thumping ended, and a plaintive voice began a song of heartbreak.

"Yes. We've even gone on a couple of dates. We've had some real arguments on those dates. I'll point out that he's being controlling, and he argues that he isn't. He's trying though. On the last date he was terribly quiet and waited for me to make the first move in everything. That was as bad as him making all the decisions. We're supposed to go in for marriage counseling in a few weeks. What about you, Jewell? How are you doing?"

"Well, up until the trail ride I was happy. Great job, great boss, despite what he's like as a husband; great horse."

"And then?"

"I ran into someone at the trail ride that claims to have been my case manager when I was twelve. She said I was in a foster home because of something my father had done. It has stirred up vague memories, and is giving me nightmares."

"Alyson is a great therapist, if you're interested."

"I don't know when I'd be able to go. I don't want to miss work."

"She has evening hours." Sara rummaged in her purse and withdrew a business card. "Here. Give her a call."

"Thanks." I stuck the card in my purse just as a familiar, masculine voice greeted us.

"Evenin' ladies."

I had to look twice before I recognized him. "Marshall?"

"Forgot me already? That's not a good sign."

I laughed to cover my nervousness. His biceps were startling. "I didn't recognize you without the cowboy hat and boots. Sara, this is Marshall...uh?"

"Provost. Howdy Ma'am. Are you ladies in the mood to dance?"

"I think I can handle it. Do you mind Sara?"

"Not at all. Go."

"Actually Sara, I have a friend with me that would like to dance also."

43

"Well, I don't know."

"He's a wonderful dancer."

"You've danced with him?"

Marshall laughed. "That's a good one. Come on then. Decide for yourself."

Justin Hughes was a good dancer, funny and gentlemanly. I wanted to sit back and watch their exchange but Marshall kept me occupied.

"I hear you've done pretty well showing Hudson in dressage."

"Yes. I'm pleased. He's way beyond me, though. Arielle is working with me to get my skills up to his level."

"When's your next show?"

"This weekend in Peoria. I usually travel with Sherry and Roger. We're showing about every weekend."

"Going to get your own trailer eventually?"

"No need at this point. Sherry has space in hers. I help with gas, so it works out for everyone. Maybe by the time my circumstances change, I'll have enough saved."

"Have any other hobbies?"

"I don't really have time for anything else. I do read. How about you?"

"Photography. You should let me shoot you with Hudson."

"I'd love that."

"Alright then."

"If photography is just a hobby, what do you do for work, Marshall?"

"I'm in real estate. In fact, Justin and I are celebrating tonight. We finally found him a place. It took awhile. He was really picky."

"Where is it?"

"Here in Groveport. That's why we're celebrating here. He wanted to start spending his money in his new hometown right away."

"Sounds like a good idea to me."

"When are you going to start house shopping?"

I laughed. "I've got a long time before I'll be in a position to buy a house. Maybe I'll never make that leap. They're a lot of work. I'd rather call the landlord and then head for the stables."

"Ah, a woman with priorities. I like that."

The show at Peoria was under a pewter sky. Arielle and Lori had already gathered their points in upper level dressage Friday afternoon. Cross country competition was all day in the fields while the lower levels of dressage occupied the outdoor arenas, and the lower levels of arena jumping utilized the indoor arena.

I got up the nerve to compete in a novice jump class in the early hours of the day and took a first place ribbon. It was Hudson's panache that did it, I was sure. He didn't try to show off by over jumping. He gauged the jumps and flew over them with only inches to spare. He simply made us look good. He still had energy for the afternoon dressage class and didn't disappoint me there either.

I had bathed the sweat off Hudson and was walking him to let him air dry, and to keep him from going down for a roll in the dirt. He was grabbing wisps of grass wherever he found a few blades as we strolled toward grassy knolls just beyond the parking lot. At the very edge he dropped his head and tore at the greenery. I leaned my body against his shiny hide; inhaled the aroma of a clean horse, and felt the softness of his hair against my cheek and bare arms.

"Oh, Hudson, what you do for me."

He turned his head to whuff in my face. The smell of crushed grass filled my nose and the blades sticking out of his mouth tickled my lips. Hudson dropped his head for another mouthful. I reached up to pinch his withers as another horse might have used its teeth for a mutual scratch.

"Look this way."

My right hand still on Hudson, I looked over my right shoulder to see who had sneaked up on us. I heard the click of a camera. It was Marshall.

"That was a great pose. I'm glad you looked over your right shoulder instead of turning around."

"Hey. You should have come earlier and got us in our show attire."

He was dressed in casual slacks and a polo shirt. I was busy looking him up and down, and up again.

"I did. Now it's time for the more personal shots."

"You got our show pictures? I didn't see you."

"I didn't want to break your concentration. I used a fifteen hundred lens."

"So how was your week? Sell a lot of houses?"

Marshall was squatting, fiddling with his camera, aiming it at me, fiddling some more.

"It was good. Sold not a one, but half the job is matching people with the perfect place. Sometimes people want places that are far bigger than they need or can handle. I try to steer them to what they'll not regret later."

"Wow. That vision must have earned you quite a clientele."

"It has. And that's what makes my job so enjoyable."

A horse whinnied in the distance. Hudson raised his head and pricked his ears. I looked at his profile in admiration and heard the camera click, whirr as it advanced, click and whirr again.

I looked at him in surprise. "I didn't know you were going to do that."

"Some of the best shots are spontaneous. A photographer has to be ready at all times."

"You didn't look ready."

Marshall just chuckled. "I was."

"You're quite a chameleon. The man in the tight muscle shirt I saw last Sunday night was so different from the cowboy at the trail ride, and different still, from the urbane photographer I see now."

He laughed. "I try to fit in no matter what setting. It puts people at ease if you can blend in with them."

I was rubbing Hudson's shoulder and pinching him along the crest of his neck. He swung his head toward me in pleasure. I lowered mine and we met forehead to forehead. The camera clicked and whirred.

"What is it about horses and women?" asked Marshall.

"They're beautiful and powerful. They give us confidence and wings to fly. I think they enjoy our gentleness and that we engage them emotionally. I think guys are more rough and tumble with them." I guiltily thought of Angel's dangerous races as I spoke.

"What do you mean, 'wings to fly'?"

"People and life can beat us down and hold us back. But if we can learn to harness horse power, it gives us confidence; shows us we can be strong and disciplined as opposed to the soft, weak, submissive creatures men want us to be."

"I don't think all men want 'soft, weak, submissive'. I find horse power pretty sexy."

I turned to give Marshall a smile. Hudson also raised his head to look at him, as if to ask if he was for real. The camera clicked and whirred catching our side by side head shot. The day suddenly seemed bright despite the overcast sky.

Alyson Moriarity was a tiny woman. She was under five feet tall and thin. For some reason, she reminded me of a wren; small, cheerful, focused on the business at hand.

"What brings you here?" she asked.

"Nightmares and lack of memories."

"Any memories."

"No. I ran into someone claiming to have been my case manager when I was twelve and in foster care. Since then, I have vague memories but nothing clear. And nightmares of sinister visitors."

"Did she give you anymore information?"

"Only that after what my father did, money was provided for my foster parents to get me psychological help which they obviously did not."

"Did this case manager identify herself?"

"Gloria Simmons."

"Is she still a case manager?"

"She didn't say."

"Where did you run into her?"

"At a trail ride in Montaine."

"How old are you now, Jewel?"

"Thirty-three."

"That's a long time to carry such a heavy secret."

"I didn't know I was carrying it. Is that possible?"

"Indeed it is. Usually it comes out in other dangerous or addictive behavior."

"I was riding horses over dangerous terrain for a while. Then I married a controlling man that made me quit. I was thinking the other day, maybe that's why I married him. I wasn't ready to die, but I couldn't stop myself from needing that rush. So I needed him to stop me. Then I divorced him because he was so controlling and I was suffocating. I'm so ashamed that I used him like that."

"That was a healthy thing to recognize, even subconsciously, that you needed help to curb your addiction to danger. It's also a healthy sign that you realize you used him. It shows growth. Jewel, what do you want from therapy?"

"I want the nightmares to stop and I want to enjoy horseback riding without the fear that I'll slip back into doing careless, dangerous things with them."

"Are you riding now?"

"Yes."

"Are you doing careless, dangerous things?"

"Well, it's wise to realize just being around horses can be dangerous. And I've just started showing in jumping classes. I'd like to eventually try cross country."

"Is that what you were doing before?"

"Kind of, but on a more extreme level. It was over very rough terrain, down steep inclines, over gullies at high speeds."

"And that's different from cross country in what way?"

"You need to be more controlled in cross country. You only speed up between jumps. Or maybe there isn't much difference and that's what worries me. Maybe I'm only a step away from where I was before."

"Do you enjoy horseback jumping?"

"Oh yes. It's how I imagine flying to be."

"Did you enjoy the rough riding?"

"No. I was terrified."

"Then why did you do it?"

"I don't know. Maybe to please a woman who had befriended me. She was the one who introduced me to the sport. Maybe for that rush of adrenaline. Possibly to prove to myself that I was fearless. Or maybe to convince myself if I could handle it, then I could handle anything."

Damascus, where Alyson was located, was a two hour drive south of Montaine. It made for a long day. Luckily, Alyson let me fill the Monday, seven o'clock slot weekly. It was another evening away from Hudson. I made up for it by riding longer in the evenings I did go to Phoenix. We rode the cross country trails while there was plenty of light. We next worked in the outdoor arena under the lights and finally finished in the indoor arena. Muscles that thought they were fit suddenly felt sore again. Lungs burned with the extra exertion. Hudson breezed through it with hardly a flared nostril. During cool down, he'd prance as though asking, "Is this the best you can do?"

Wednesday was still my downtime night, and this Wednesday, I was glad. It had been a horrendously challenging day at work. Brad seemed to be angry and was pushing us hard. He and Greg had even had loud words over some issue within the confines of his office. I heard the volume, if not what was actually said.

I wondered if his mood had something to do with his relationship with Sara. Or maybe, he had decided to help Courtney financially and needed to increase business. What ever the reason, I was leaving work exhausted in the evenings. Surprisingly, after a couple hours with Hudson, I'd feel rejuvenated. I was giving him lots of hugs, but Hudson seemed impatient with those. It was almost as if he was saying, "If you loved, me you'd spend more time in the saddle," although my muscles claimed I was doing just that.

This Wednesday I was glad it was downtime night. I dragged myself into my apartment and dropped into the armchair. Maybe the fact that the nightmares were persisting in disrupting my sleep was adding to my tiredness. I was hungry but couldn't pull myself up to make anything. I dozed off and about fifteen minutes later the phone rang. I was glad I was still sitting in the chair with the phone within reach.

"Hello."

"Hello. Jewel, is that you?"

"Yeah."

"Are you alright? You don't sound your normal self."

"Just tired. What's up, Madison?"

"Marshall wants to bring over your pictures. I hope you don't mind. He showed them to us and they are spectacular. I hope you'll let us post one of your show pictures on our bulletin board and in our newsletter. Anyway, we never give out phone numbers or addresses but I told him I'd give you a call to see if he could bring them by."

I was sitting up straight now. "Sure. I'm anxious to see them."

"Here, I'll let you give him directions."

"Jules, this is Marshall. Have you eaten?"

"No and I'm famished."

"Do you like oriental?"

"General Tsao's"

"Great. Give me directions and I'm on my way."

I was suddenly energized. I utilized his travel time to shower and change into fresh clothes. My hair wasn't quite dry before the doorbell rang. Barefoot, in shorts and tank top, I opened the door. "Hey."

I saw his eyes swoop downward and back up taking me all in. "I should have brought the camera."

I let the remark slide without a response. "Plates?"

"Naw" We can eat out of the box."

Two hours later, leaving me with a set of prints, he left with an order for three enlargements. Marshall had liked our head shot so I ordered an eight by ten of it to give to him as a gift. I also ordered an eight by ten of our forehead to forehead pose as well as an eleven by fourteen of Hudson and me sailing over a jump. I found a "thinking of you" card from the stock I kept on hand, slid in a print of Hudson and me accepting the first place ribbon for our jump class and wrote a short note to Angel before sealing it.

Thursday morning at the fitness club, I was just finishing my cool down on the treadmill and heading for the showers, when I saw Sara leaving the office. She saw me and waved.

"I decided to follow your example. I need to firm up these sags and bags."

"Good for you. How did your "couples" session with Alyson go? That was Tuesday, right?"

"Yes, it was, but it didn't go well. Brad claims wanting to be in control is part of being a man and a lawyer. He said he's very frustrated trying to change and I should accept his control in exchange for the 'good life' he's provided. I said I had accepted it for twenty-two years. Now I want control over my own life. So I guess we aren't dating anymore."

"Divorce?"

"Well, I haven't filed and I haven't been served papers from him, so I'll wait a bit. Let him think over what he said. Until then, I'm moving ahead with my life."

"How are Heather and Brooke doing?"

"Brooke is becoming very withdrawn, especially so when she comes back from visits with her father. I'm starting to get worried about her. Heather says she loves her father but she's not ever going to marry, have a brat like Brooke, or give up control of her life in any way."

"Poor Brooke. Well, I must get to work, Sara. Have a good day."

"Will I see you here in the morning?"

"I'll be here."

Thursday evening, when I arrived at Phoenix, there seemed to be a somber atmosphere hanging over everyone and several stable hands wore black armbands. I was wondering what had happened as I walked past the bulletin board and saw a large picture of an old man on one of the saddle club horses. A long black-lettered banner proclaimed: 'In Remembrance of Clint Flowers.'

I saw Josie on her way to the arena with a student. "Josie, is this the Clint Flowers that started the Saddle Club?"

"Yes. It's to help troubled kids keep from going bad. I suppose you saw the saddle club van bringing in the kids in the evenings? They pretty much keep to the back stables and arenas when they're here. He was a really close friend of Madison's. He passed away early this morning. He was doing a wonderful thing with those kids. Saved a lot of them from getting into trouble. A few have even gone on to college on scholarships Clint set up."

"Who's going to run it now?"

"John Smith had helped Clint get it up and going. As Clint got older, John took over more and more of the program. He's a policeman in Montaine. Madison oversees it, of course. They're always looking for more mentors so if you know anyone…."

"I'll keep it in mind."

Hudson and I were soon headed for the cross country course. I was riding it in reverse direction so it would look different to Hudson. For some reason, the obstacles looked scarier to me, but Hudson seemed to hardly notice.

CHAPTER EIGHT

I was leaving Alyson's office deep in thought. She had suggested trying to track down Gloria Simmons and hopefully go back to my foster parents for a visit looking for something to jog the memory. The only way I knew to get in contact with her would be through the Phoenix mail list. I couldn't expect Shelly to give me Gloria's phone number, but hoped she'd pass my number onto her, so she could call me if she wanted to help. I could only ask.

As I stepped out from the building, I plowed into someone passing the entrance.

"Oh, excuse me," I stammered as I looked up at the blond hair and deep blue eyes set in a young face.

At first she had a scowl, perturbed at being bumped. Her eyes shifted to the sign by the door I had just exited, and the scowl slid into a smirk as a snigger escaped her blood red lips.

"Jules, are you alright?"

I looked at the man next to her. My face blushed hot with shame. "I'm fine," I said, hearing my voice crack with embarrassment. I looked at the woman. "I'm sorry. I wasn't watching where I was going."

I hurried away, my heart beating fiercely, my breath refusing to come until I was around the corner and then it came in sobs. I worked at getting it under control as I threaded my way through the people on the sidewalk who threw curious glances my way. I ducked into a small diner to escape the stares. I slid into a booth and finally got control of my body.

A waitress was instantly at my table, placing a menu before me. "Would you like something to drink?"

"Do you have herbal teas?" I sniffed, keeping my red rimmed eyes on the napkin dispenser.

"I'm afraid not."

"Well, just a regular tea then. No, make it a decaf coffee."

I quickly scanned the menu. I didn't want anything to eat, but I wanted an excuse to sit for awhile. She returned with my coffee and I ordered a piece of carrot cake. It came. I let it sit untouched while my hands found calmness from the warmth of the coffee cup they curled around. I stared out the plate glass window, watching people passing, intent on their own lives. I couldn't help wonder how many of them visited a psychologist to help them with their demons, or how many of them loved someone who loved someone else.

My eyes wanted to tear up. I bit my lips to keep them from quivering. Again, my thoughts became turbulent over the shame of the New Life Psychological Center sign that the young woman sniggered at, and the pain of seeing Marshall with that same young woman. What was I crying about? He had never indicated any commitment to me. Just because he brightened my life didn't mean he was serious about me. He was free to date anyone he chose. I was certain he wouldn't choose a mental patient. I felt my hope drop dead. I had to get out of the diner. The tears were flowing and I couldn't get them stopped. I left a ten dollar bill on the table and stumbled out the door, located my car, and headed home.

The highway stretched out in a blur before me. To my left, streaks of gold and orange lay close to the horizon. I kept looking at the brush strokes of color for the strength to stop the tears. Each time I glanced back to the road my car traveled, however, I noticed a huge black cloud covering the highway. It seemed to reach to the ground. Even though I was driving on dry pavement, I realized what

I saw was a wall of rain. The cars ahead of me each disappeared as though swallowed by a monster.

It seemed surreal as I approached the purple wall. I took one last look at the bright splashes of color, low in the western sky. Grey clouds with bright underbellies scudded just above the bright swaths created by the sun's rays. Fat, heavy drops of rain suddenly hit my windshield. The tires hissed on the wet pavement as I entered the blinding downpour. The visibility became non-existent. In panic, I felt my foot jump from the gas pedal toward the brake as the red eyes of the monster focused on me and I felt the flashes of pain as it bit down on my body.

Pain was my first sensation as I gained a measure of consciousness. I heard myself groaning; heard a voice calling my name; struggled to rise up out of oblivion; finally opened my eyes in a pastel room full of natural light. I squinted and tried to look around, but flashes of pain cautioned me against movement. I wanted to tell the voice calling my name that I hurt, but my tongue felt thick and dry, so I tried to say "water" instead. I felt the wet sponge-on-a-stick wipe my tongue and the insides of my cheeks. I couldn't ignore the throbbing produced by the small accomplishment of swallowing that tiny bit of moisture into my parched body.

"I hurt," I finally managed to rasp.

"I'll bet you do. That was quite a pile up. Do you remember what happened?"

She was just a blur of white moving about my body closing the IV tubing to flow a bit slower; injecting a dose of something through an IV port; checking my urine output in the urine bag hanging at the side of the bed; getting a warm cloth to not-so-gently wipe my face, seeming to hardly care about the bruises. I was trying to remember, but the sun on my face, and the comfort of the dose of the pain-killing drug soothed me back into oblivion.

The spans of wakefulness increased, and the moments of lucidity grew longer. I gradually remembered the purple-grey monster, whose red eyes were actually the tail lights of the car that had been traveling ahead of me; the bite of the monster was actually a six car accident, whose drivers were unprepared for the instant change in visibility. And then I also remembered the reason I had been crying, which is why I was totally surprised when Marshall joined the visitors to my hospital room.

"Hey," he said softly. "How are you?"

He added his name to my leg casts and drew a smiley face on my arm cast. I couldn't help smiling but I tried hard to keep my heart from fluttering and my mind from humming 'Ode to Joy'.

"The doctors say I'm doing great. I can probably go home in a couple days."

"Do you need a ride?"

"I was going to ask Sara if she could help."

"Let me. I'm sure my schedule is more flexible than hers, and it'll be easier for me to get you up the stairs to your apartment."

"Alright. Do you know anything about my car?"

"Pretty much totaled."

I tried not to react. My problems weren't Marshall's concerns. I would not burden him with them.

Discharge day arrived. I had to admit I was nervous. I was not at all sure how I would navigate the challenges ahead: getting groceries, doing laundry, work, caring for Hudson. My head was spinning with the enormity of it and I could hardly focus on the instructions from the doctor.

"Start moving around as much as possible but don't overtax your self."

There was a knock at the door. Marshall entered pushing a wheelchair. "Your chariot, m'lady."

"Alright then," continued the doctor. "Don't forget your first appointment with Dr. Holloway a week from today."

Marshall pulled the wheelchair, with me in it, backwards up the stairs to my apartment as if it was nothing. The furniture had all been pushed back against the walls, so there was room to maneuver the wheelchair. There was a stack of library books on the end table. He showed me the paper plates and plastic ware that would cut down on clean up. Pot's and pans, as well as easy to prepare boxed foods, were stacked on the counter. He opened the refrigerator to reveal fresh fruit, veggies and drinks.

"That should keep you for a few days, don't you think?"

"Marshall, did you do this?"

"Your support system, of which I am a part, did."

Tears sprang to my eyes.

I was amazed at how many friends were helping me. Arielle said she'd ride Hudson to keep him in shape for me. I felt I was imposing on her, but I was so grateful and relieved. I had called Brad to give him an idea of a time table for my return to work. He had asked if there was anything he could do and I had chuckled nervously as I suggested he hold my job for me. He didn't say he would. I called Sara to see if she could help me when it was time to get more groceries. She assured me she would help where needed. She volunteered Heather's services with cleaning whenever I wanted. I called Alyson and told her I'd not be in for several weeks. She again suggested I should use the time to try to contact Gloria Simmons and my former foster parents to see if they could enlighten my past. I asked Shelly if she could contact Gloria for me. Gloria returned the call within a few days and said she'd ask the foster parents if they'd agree to a meeting.

I read the books Marshall had gotten for me from the library. I slept. Sara came every morning to help me bathe and get into a clean gown or into clothes for my doctor visits. She took my soiled clothes and brought them back laundered and folded. Heather came to tidy up for me. Arielle dropped in for a chat about her approaching day to leave for college, an update on Hudson, and occasionally had time to play a hand of cards or a board game. Marshall dropped in every couple days to check up on me, take out the trash, and visit for a couple hours. He was the one who got me up and down the stairs for my doctor visits, and a few times he took me to Phoenix afterward to see Hudson. I called Angel and we talked like old friends. She showed up the next day with pizza and several DVDs for a movie marathon.

By the fourth week in the casts, I was rolling in and out of bed pretty good on my own. I could one handedly bathe and slip a gown over my head. That was also the week Gloria brought Mr. and Mrs. Melesky for a visit.

The moment I saw them, the memories tugged at the edges of my consciousness. They were good memories of a town called Hoverdale, of learning to ride horses, swimming, and playing softball. They brought albums of pictures showing me in the many activities, and posing with their daughters: Hannah, Dee Dee and Sidney. They apologized for skipping the psychotherapy, but said I was doing so well, they thought I didn't need it. They had put the money toward the cost of sending me to summer camp that year. They left me their phone number and an invitation to call and visit. They explained, Hoverdale was about an hour to the west of Montaine. Sidney was the only daughter living in Hoverdale. Dee Dee lived to the south in Augusta, and Hannah resided northward in Drummond.

I asked Gloria what exactly my father had done. She answered that he had raped me and murdered my mother when she had tried to intervene. He died in a brawl in the prison where he had been serving out his sentence. I felt nothing over his death, neither sorrow nor glee, but I did get a chill at a vague, ugly memory of the excruciating pain of forced sex, of yelling, flying fists, splattered blood, and the loneliness of drawing so deep within myself, I was sure no one could ever hurt me again.

I was agitated that evening when Marshall dropped in.

He asked with concern on his face. "Are you okay?"

"Not really. Today I had visitors from my past. They were my foster parents long ago. They were nice. I hope to visit them when I'm able, but I also found out why I was in foster care to begin with, and that was disturbing.

"Need a visit to your therapist?"

My face flushed at the remembrance of that day. I laughed nervously. "I was so embarrassed to be found out by you and your friend that day."

"What's to be embarrassed about? And Christine was a client, not a friend. We had just closed on a condo I had found for them. Her husband was ahead of us picking up some tickets to a ball game at the ticket master."

I felt a warmth flood through me like a spring rain. I couldn't help the smile that sprouted like a flower on my face as I responded, "Is that right?"

CHAPTER NINE

The casts came off, revealing white, wrinkled limbs. Despite the extreme high summer temperatures, if I went out, I donned jeans and a thin, long-sleeved cotton shirt to hide the light and air-starved skin. I had a check from the insurance company in the bank. From the cast-removal appointment, Marshall was taking me out to see Hudson and then car shopping. I also needed to call Brad to see about starting back to work.

My legs quickly fatigued from standing next to Hudson, and my arms ached as I tried to groom him. I leaned against him to rest, and then groomed some more. Although he stood still for grooming, he was a lot of horse under saddle. I knew I'd need to build up my strength before getting on him again. Afterwards, we found a used, fire engine red Stratus priced within my budget limits.

"How about carry out and a movie?" asked Marshall, before I got behind the wheel of my new vehicle.

"Sounds great."

"I'll stop and get it on the way. Then I'll coach you at squats and push ups."

I laughed. "Not just yet. But I will start back to the gym and start gently. First I need to call Brad and let him know I can start back to work."

"Okay. I'll meet you at your place."

"Gee, I'm sorry Jules," said Brad, " but this girl Friday has worked out really great. I hired her and don't really need two secretaries. I didn't actually terminate you while you were on your leave so you'd have the insurance. But now that you're able to work again, I'll have to cancel it."

The words hit me like a kick from an angry horse. I felt the blood drain from my face.

"I can write you a reference letter," he added.

"Thanks," I managed to reply although it was barely above a whisper. I set the receiver down just as Marshall entered the door with our meal in his hands. My face must have still revealed my shock.

"Jules, what's wrong?"

"I don't have a job. I know it was six weeks but….Do you think it's because I'm friends with Sara? I never let that interfere with my work."

"Boy, that is a shock."

"I'll have to sell Hudson. I can't afford boarding fees."

Tears welled in my eyes. I was frightened and angry. Hudson was one of the best things that had ever happened to me, but being unemployed with financial obligations made me tremble.

"Whoa, whoa. There are other positions; other lawyers; a whole world full of job opportunities."

"But it may take awhile to find another."

Marshall came to me, put his hands on my upper arms and rubbed up and down. "Hey, it's going to be all right. Try to see it as a redirection of your life. Maybe there's a better job out there waiting for you to find it. Things will be even better. You'll see."

"I don't know…."

"Come on, show me some of that horse power."

I gave a weak smile.

"Are you going to be able to enjoy this movie, or should we start an internet job search?"

I wanted to start searching right away. My gut was churning, and I felt dizzy with the fear of being jobless, but his challenge to show him some horse power made me swallow and say, "Movie and a meal. I'll start searching in the morning."

I started the next morning by going to the fitness center to swim. I tried to keep my mind reviewing what I wanted in my life, as Marshall had recommended the night before. I wanted Hudson there, but I vacillated between believing I could have him, and fearing I was going to lose him. I was so glad Angel had paid for a years worth of boarding for him, although at the time I had secretly thought she was being incredibly free with my money.

I ran into Sara in the locker room.

"Welcome back. When are you starting back to work?" she queried."

"As soon as I find a job."

"Excuse me?"

"Brad didn't hold my job."

"Jewel, I'm so sorry."

"It's not your fault."

"Probably it is. He knows we're friends, and things aren't good between him and me."

I simply shrugged my shoulders.

It was a beautiful sunny morning with not a cloud in the sky and very little humidity. After my swim, I wanted to go out to see Hudson, but thought maybe I should give my muscles a rest while sending out resume's over the internet, and go to Phoenix later. I just got in the door of my apartment when the phone rang.

"Hello."

"Jewel? This is Sidney Melesky." The voice was high and tight with excitement. "I just found out that Mom and Dad had been to visit you! Oh my gosh, I can't believe you're back in our lives. We're planning a welcome back party. Please say you'll come. There are so many people who want to see you."

"That's really nice of you. When is it?"

"We thought we'd let you pick a day convenient for you."

"Right now, I'm jobless, so unless my fairy godmother visits within the next week, I'm free any time."

Sidney gasped. "You mean just until your casts come off, right?"

"They're off. I called my old boss to let him know I could come back to work but he had hired someone else."

"The PRICK."

I chuckled nervously. "I have a friend that says there's a better job waiting for me and this had to happen so I could make room for it in my life."

"I like that philosophy. How about next Sunday afternoon, in case you have interviews during the week."

"Sounds good to me. Can you give me directions?"

By afternoon, I was discouraged and ready to head for Phoenix. I was thrilled that Arielle was there giving a lesson. We waved and after giving the class a command to walk their mounts, she came to where I was watching.

"I heard you were back. How's it feel?"

"Weak, actually. I'd like to ride but I don't figure I'll last long. I know I've imposed on you an awful lot, but if you aren't busy after your class, could you give Hudson a good work out after I give out?"

"I'd love to."

I sighed in relief. "Thanks Arielle. I really owe you for all you've done."

She laughed. "I owe you for all the experience you've allowed me to garner from riding him."

"I'm sure going to miss you when you leave for college. Are you busy this evening or can you come for dinner? We need a girl's night in before you leave."

"Actually tonight would be perfect."

I groomed Hudson. He seemed to realize I was going to ride and found it difficult to stand still.

"I'm not as strong as I once was Hud. Take it easy on me, okay?" He nodded his head and whuffled in my face. I laughed, and wondered if he really understood me.

I stretched his legs and mounted up. He walked with animation. Despite Arielle's working him while I was laid up, I could tell he wanted to be anything but sedate.

I couldn't post the trot for very long. Sweat beaded on my brow. I had to keep taking him back to the walk to rest myself. I could feel the energy building up in Hudson's body and thought he was going to explode. I wanted so much to let him use that energy but then I remembered a well-trained horse must be calm and controlled.

"This will be a perfect training session for you, big boy."

With that shift in attitude from a tense, holding him in, to a more relaxed hold of the reins, my body seemed to settle into an expectation-of-control mode. Hudson immediately settled to the task of walking in a gentlemanly fashion.

Arielle's class of giggling girls was over. I heard them ohhing and ahhing over progress they had made, and moaning over sore muscles, as they led their mounts to the grooming bays. Arielle came my way.

"I saw that. That was great."

"Saw what?"

"How you settled him down; made him walk like a man instead of an explosive juvenile."

"That was good?"

"That was awesome. Do you want to make that the whole lesson?"

"I'd rather reward him with some hard work." I dismounted and held out the reins. "I'll wait here to cool him out and groom after you bring him back. Is there anything I can do for you while you're doing this favor for me?"

"Can you help bring in the horses from pasture?"

"Sure."

I had roast chicken and a pasta salad made by the time Arielle got to my place that evening. She brought the green tea and peach sherbet for dessert.

"So where are you going to school?"

"Erie."

"To major in what?"

"Horse management. I want to know the whole thing. Training, stable management, showing, husbandry."

"You already know all of it except maybe the husbandry."

"That's what Madison says too."

"So why go?"

"I don't know. Maybe I want a certificate on the wall to prove I know it."

"I'll make you a certificate," I laughed. "School will just give you loans you'll have to repay. I think you should just get a job. I'm sure Madison would write you a glowing reference letter."

"Madison said that also. I guess I just think it would be easier to get a business loan and clients if I could prove I know it."

"As well known as you are on the show circuit, I still think you don't need it. But I do understand your reasoning."

"Besides, I promised my parents I'd go to college and get a liberal education. They're worried that I can't make a livelihood on horses."

"I can understand that, also. Too bad there isn't a college close by you could attend part time so you could continue to work with horses. And I wish there was something I could do to help you."

Arielle smiled. "You have. You've given me experience on Hudson."

"So you've said."

Between swimming and riding Hudson, I could feel my body rapidly gaining strength. I added the treadmill and upper body machines to my routine and struggled home exhausted. I had interviews set up in Damascus and Groveport. I had had one interview in Montaine but it would be a pay cut and I didn't want to go backwards.

Marshall called Wednesday. "How about a day at the lake on Sunday?"

For a moment it crossed my mind to cancel on the family's party so I could go with Marshall, but they were so excited about it, and frankly so was I. "I'm sorry Marshall. The Melesky's are having a party for me on Sunday. It's a welcome-back-into-their-life party."

"That's wonderful. You'll have a great time. We'll catch the lake another day if the weather holds."

"I'd love that."

"Okay then, I'll call you next week sometime."

"Looking forward to it."

Sunday dawned overcast and humid. I had butterflies in my stomach while dressing and driving to Hoverdale. I couldn't even get myself to eat a light breakfast. The countryside was beautiful on the way and I soon forgot my nervousness as I enjoyed the scenery. The further I traveled toward Hoverdale the sunnier it got. I thought it was a good sign.

The directions were easy. I was soon pulling into the drive. I was shocked at the number of cars parked in the yard in front of the house and along the drive. I thought I should park at the very end of the line of parked vehicles, but saw someone dash out the front door and frantically wave me forward. I rolled my window down as I got closer.

"Hi, Jewel. You haven't changed a bit. We saved you a spot right in front of the garage."

I smiled, recognizing the high, tight voice of Sidney. "Thanks. That was sweet of you."

"Well, you are the guest of honor."

"I didn't expect so many people here."

Sidney laughed. "Neither did we."

She hooked her left arm through my right arm as we walked around the house to the back yard. I was soon drowning in a sea of faces that converged on me with the sound of an ocean roar. I felt another arm link through my left. Mrs. Melesky and Sidney held me upright as we slowly made our way through the crowd. They introduced me to each individual and gave the history of how they were related to, or involved with the family. I tried to smile and focus on each face before me, but the stories crashed and foamed and then ebbed away to forgetfulness. Every now and again I noticed one woman just watching; not making any effort to get close. Her calm scrutiny gave me goose bumps.

Finally, the chaos subsided. As the crowd around me thinned, I breathed easier. The waves of people settled into tidal pools here and there. I found a lawn chair in which to sit, relax and watch. Two gas grills were fired up. There were kids in the pool, teens playing bad mitten, guys playing a game of football, toddlers chasing dogs, dogs barking and playing tag with each other.

A standard poodle trotted to me. She sat close and leaned in against my leg, her soulful eyes rolling up at me. Many of the women had gone into the house to start carrying out the food to set on the picnic tables. I felt I should be helping and was just about to get up when she appeared to block my way. I had to shield my eyes from the sun to look up at her.

"This isn't what Mom had planned for you." She sat in the lawn chair next to me. "Hi. I'm Hannah."

There was the face, now open and friendly instead of locked in concentration. Her hair was thick waves of brunette with slight premature graying at the temples. The long tresses fell over bare, tanned arms that set off her yellow sun dress. Her wrists were circled by dainty bracelets, and her ringed fingers were long and elegant.

"Hello, Hannah. I'm not sure but I think you're one of the first I was actually suppose to meet today."

"Sidney was so excited about you coming back into our lives, she couldn't keep her mouth shut. I guess we'll have to forgive her."

"Were we close?"

"You weren't emotionally close to anyone but Sidney thought she was your savior. Maybe some of it was because you were both the same age. For whatever the reason, she really worked at drawing you out. I think she's so excited because she thinks any success you've had is a reflection of her efforts."

"Who knows? Maybe it is. What about our relationship?"

"I watched you a lot, but Sidney was in your face so much, I didn't think you needed anymore," she chuckled. "You were so focused on whatever you did, I had the feeling you weren't really aware of us. You got straight A's throughout school, you got scads of ribbons at horse shows, you played a mean game of soft ball, and were a swimming champion. I guess if Sidney hadn't dragged you to each of those activities, you'd have hidden behind a book in your room. It's strange; those were all Sidney's activities also. You out shown her in all of them and yet she never seemed to mind. She was so proud of you, like she was your mother or something. Your senior year, you had a boyfriend. He was a geek but seemed sweet. You really blossomed then."

"What was his name?"

"You don't remember? It was Fisher Price. How sad is that?"

"Fisher," I murmured. "I do remember him. He was my boyfriend?"

"It appeared so to us, and to him as well, I think. He was heartbroken when you left without leaving him a way to contact you. I could probably find his picture in a high school yearbook."

I didn't answer so she continued. "You so fascinated me, however, that I did become a psychiatrist."

"I'm not sure if that's a complement or an insult."

"It needn't be either. It's just a statement. We never know how we'll affect other people. I'm glad you affected me that way. I've had a very fulfilling life."

"No husband or kids?"

"No. I don't feel the need. And none of the guys I've dated made me feel they'd be a positive addition to my life."

"What does Sidney do?"

"She's married to Bob Campbell, attorney at law. Spends her days working out at the gym, shopping and making sure Bob's life runs smoothly and that she looks good on his arm."

"Poor girl. She should have at least been a mother."

"Yes, indeed," Hannah solemnly concurred.

The big curly dog laid her head on my thigh. I absently scratched her behind her ears and massaged her neck. Hannah was watching my hand on the dog.

"And Dee Dee? I haven't seen her yet."

"You probably have. You've just been overwhelmed and she's considerate enough to let you catch your breath. She's a writer. Has three published novels under her belt; working on a fourth. Lots of short stories published in between chapters and occasional feature articles to help keep change in the coffers."

"That has to be stressful, always worrying about money."

"I'm not sure she worries about it."

"I do. I'm terrified to be jobless."

"How's the search coming along?"

"There's one in Montaine but it would be a pay cut. I could do it, but it would be more difficult. I interviewed in Damascus, but that's a two hour commute or relocation. I really like the people where I board CastleontheHudson. I'd miss them if I'd relocate." My mind thought of Marshall as I said it, but I kept that to myself. "I'm seriously thinking about the one in Groveport. It's forty minutes east. The pay is about the same as I was making, but I got a creepy feeling while I was interviewing. There wasn't anything wrong that I could put my finger on; just that feeling in my gut."

"Listen to it. Don't even question it. Just don't take that job."

"You really believe in hunches?"

"I really do."

We were both watching a slim woman with dark, short, spiky hair; in jean shorts and a tank top approaching. One of the dogs was bounding along at her side but as the woman neared us it stopped. As it stared at the poodle sitting next to me, its pyle rose. It skirted around us to run after a ball thrown by a young boy. The woman's smile was big and genuine. She leaned down and gave me a kiss. I saw the sparkle of a tiny diamond nose ring.

"Dee Dee?"

"Welcome back to the fold, Sis."

"Thanks. I hear you're a writer. What made you want to do that?"

"I'm a control freak."

"Excuse me?"

"It's the only place I have any control over outcomes. If someone has a rough life, I can give her a happy ending. If she's a shrew, I can give her what she deserves."

I laughed. "That would be satisfying."

The poodle had lain down with its muzzle resting across my foot. Sidney was coming our way pulling a tall man that might once have been athletic but was now going soft. It looked as if he were scowling but as they drew closer his eyes rested on me and widened. His mouth curved upward and the creases between his brows disappeared.

"Jewel, this is Bob, my husband. I told him he has to give you a job."

"That's nice of you Sidney, but I wouldn't impose on him like that."

"Now don't discard the offer too quickly," said Bob. "I could at least give you an interview. You're a lot prettier than that picture Sid showed me. You were quite a homely kid." His eyes shifted over my body.

"So, if you thought I was still homely, you wouldn't interview me?"

The dog at my feet sat up, once again leaning against my leg and placing herself between Bob and me. I heard nothing but felt the vibration of a growl through her ribs.

"Well, good looks help. Pleasant scenery make my days easier."

Sidney punched his arm but her voice raised a pitch. "He's only kidding."

The drive home was filled with guilt. They had all tried so hard to make me feel welcome in their lives and I was eager to get to know them again. Even the big poodle had sat at the end of the drive and watched me leave. Sidney wanted me to move to Hoverdale.

"You can stable Hudson in Dad's barn. That'll save you a pretty penny."

"Hudson wouldn't be happy alone," I had replied.

"I'll get a horse and we can ride together," she said excitedly then turned to Bob for affirmation. "I can have a horse can't I sweety?"

The hair stood on the back of my neck as he answered, "Anything you need to bring Jewel back into the fold is fine with me."

Mr. Melesky added, "It'll be nice having horses around again."

If I owed any of them, it was probably Sidney. I wanted badly to repay her with friendship but that feeling in my gut that Hannah said to heed was cautioning me. The matter closed when Bob leaned close as I was leaving and whispered a figure for my salary per week. It was exorbitantly high and hinted at extra duties behind closed doors. The smirk on his face claimed I couldn't possibly pass it up, but that's exactly what I intended to do.

Mrs. Melesky gave me a hug as I left. "Please visit again."

"I will, Mom."

Tears sprang to her eyes. "That's the first time you've ever called me that."

CHAPTER TEN

I was driving home from another interview in Damascus. I tensed up as I passed through the section of highway where the accident had happened but my thoughts quickly returned to the business at hand. The interview had gone well. The pay would be good but I was troubled. I didn't know where Marshall lived. He was at the stables frequently as Madison, Shelly, Connor and John were all his friends even though he didn't ride. So he couldn't live far from Phoenix. If I moved to Damascus, I might lose contact with him. Even though he had made no declaration of love, I knew I was in love with him. I was seriously considering taking the position in Montaine just to remain close to him. The more I thought about it, the more sure I was that that was the right choice, IF the job at Stahlman, Stidd and Austin was still available. I decided to stop at the office to see if the position was still an option.

The receptionist did a double take as I walked into the waiting room. "Boy, that was fast," she said.

"What do you mean?"

"I called you not five minutes ago."

Mr. Stidd came out of his office. He waved as he came toward us and heard me say, "Oh, I haven't been at home. I just got back from an interview in Damascus."

"Miss Fitzgerald, let's go into my office for a chat, shall we?" urged Mr. Stidd. "Janice, would you get us some coffee?"

"Yes, sir."

He ushered me to a seat. "Now Miss Fitzgerald, what can we do to get you to accept the position for which we interviewed you?"

For a moment I was speechless and glad that Janice brought the coffee at that moment which gave me time to recover. "Well, the only thing that gave me pause was the pay. It's a bit less than I'm comfortable with."

"What amount would you need?"

I took a sip of the strong, hot brew to give myself time for a quick calculation. I added a dollar onto what Brad had paid me since I now considered myself experienced and figured it would give room for negotiation.

When I stated the amount, Mr. Stidd bellowed, "Done! When can you start?"

"Monday would be good for me."

"Monday it is."

As I passed Janice's desk with a smile on my face, she gave me the thumbs up.

I whispered, "What happened?"

"First, you should have seen the other women applying for the job. Nose rings; pink and blue hair. No interviewing skills at all. New grads, you know? Second, they called your old boss who gave you a glowing reference. Third, the work is piling up. So welcome aboard. When do you start?"

"Monday. See you then."

When I got home, I wrote all the other places where I had interviewed or had sent a resume to thank them for considering my application and to inform them I was no longer considering their firms for employment. Then I called Marshall.

"Are you busy?"

"Not real busy, what's up?"

"I just wanted you to know I got a job. I start Monday."

"Good for you. Which one did you take?"

"Montaine."

"I thought that one didn't pay enough?"

"There's a whole story to it. I don't want to take up too much of your time, so how about…"

"We go celebrate," Marshall cut in. "I'll pick you up at seven and you can tell me all about it."

After changing clothes, I headed for Phoenix. I was going to go for a ride worthy of Hudson's power. I felt sprinkled with star dust. It seemed euphoria buoyed me an inch above my car seat. All was well.

Hudson was in the pasture and I called his name. His head shot up, he whinnied and galloped for the gate. His excitement stirred up the other geldings that bucked, reared and galloped with him. Going in among them, I snapped on his lead and then had to shoo the others away so none would slip out as we left the pasture.

"Are you ready to work, Hud? This has been an awesome day. I am so charged."

I didn't need to tell him that. He sensed it and was prancing by my side. I knew if I didn't calm down, I couldn't expect Hudson to be calm. I started slowing and deepening my breaths. By the time I mounted, we were both in control and walked mannerly toward the trails.

I had the rest of the day to enjoy, so we walked the whole length of the trails but then we exploded onto the cross country course and worked up a sweat. Hudson was blowing and prancing, reveling in his masculinity. I let him gloat until we turned for home. Despite my aching body, we were genteel and cooled out by the time we reached the barn.

Marshall was on time. As always, he looked "executive" in suit and tie.

"Whew, you look good," he said.

"So do you," I replied. "Where to?"

"How about Dante's?"

"Sounds good."

He waited until we were on the road before saying, "So tell me the story."

The telling didn't take long. I left out the part about the fear of losing contact with him.

"Don't you think you'd make friends elsewhere?"

"I'm sure I would. But I've just rediscovered a family I didn't realize I'd mislaid, and the people at Phoenix are so awesome. I just don't think anyone could measure up to the people I'm surrounded by right now."

"Marshall reached across the console to take my hand. "Am I included in that glowing tribute?"

My heart pounded. "Yes, you are."

He smiled. "I'm glad to hear that."

When I crawled into bed that night, it was with anticipation of a day at the lake with Marshall on Sunday. My mind was aflutter with ideas for what to pack for our picnic. I wasn't going to let anything cancel that day with Marshall but there was a show on Saturday; my first since the accident. I would be participating in dressage and arena jumping, so for the next three days, I worked Hudson on those skills. Friday, I took him over the cross country course to use up energy and give him a break from the rigors of arena work.

We'd be leaving at three in the morning so I had a hot soak in the tub to relax myself and then got out the album of my childhood with the Melesky's to look through. The pictures gave me a good feeling. I especially liked the one of me lying with my head on the curly-coated standard poodle I had seen and petted at the family party. Then, shocked, I said out loud, "Wait. That was over twenty years ago. That can't be the same dog. I'll have to ask someone if the dogs are related."

At two o'clock the alarm clamored me into a slight semblance of wakefulness. I quickly dressed and drove out to Phoenix. Lights were on and people were packing foot lockers and horse trailers. I could smell the aroma of freshly brewed coffee coming from the lounge and made a mental note to grab a cup before leaving.

Sherry and I had a routine and we fell back into it as if I'd not been off the circuit for two months. We had just finished grooming our horses and packing the utensils in the foot lockers when Marshall walked in.

"Can I help with anything?"

I smiled. "I didn't expect you here."

"Wouldn't miss it. Besides, there's always pictures to take."

"Ah, yes. Can you load the foot locker? Roger can show you where to put it."

Sherry and I led our horses to the trailer. Special Package clomped up the ramp and Hudson followed close behind. Marshall appeared behind me with that cup of coffee I wanted.

"Can I give you a lift?"

I looked at Sherry.

"Go ahead," she replied to my unasked question.

"We'll follow you," Marshall said to her.

The trailer pulled out behind several others. Marshall followed. Three more trailers fell in behind to complete the convoy.

At six o'clock, we pulled into a Waffle House with big rig parking for breakfast. When we came back out, a tire on the Chandler's trailer was flat.

"You go on with Sherry and Roger. I'll help Jack and Audrey get this taken care of and get them back on the road."

We pulled onto the show grounds at eight thirty. The flat-tire gang showed up two hours later, barely in time to make their first class.

I was excited to be back into showing. Hudson's coat gleamed, his hooves glistened with polish. His head was up; eyes bright, ears pricked revealing he too was glad to be here. The air was filled with the fragrances of horse and hay, odors of saddle soap and fly repellant, the aroma of woodchips in the warm-up ring.

Hudson and I were passing the novice ring as the class was leaving. I watched as the losers worked to keep their faces neutral and the winners that couldn't do it if they tried. I saw a face I recognized.

"Brooke," I called to her.

Here eyes searched for the voice. I called again and moved Hudson closer. Her eyes finally found me. I almost cried at the sadness I saw there.

"You finally got your own horse."

"Yeah."

"Is this your first show?"

"No. I've been showing for awhile now."

"Good for you."

"Not really. I'm not doing very good."

"Well, don't give up. Be patient with yourself. Are you here with your mom?"

She shook her head and for a moment I thought she was going to cry. I sidled Hudson closer to her horse so I could reach out to put my gloved hand on her shoulder. "Are you okay?"

She nodded.

"So, spending time with Dad?"

She shook her head "no" but didn't seem to trust herself to speak.

"So what's your horse's name?"

"Rovin' Raven." Her voice cracked.

"Where are you keeping him?"

"Dad bought a small farm when…so I could have a horse."

"That was nice of him."

Brooke nodded and kicked Rovin' Raven into a trot leaving Hudson and me behind.

Marshall and I crossed paths once about noon. We grabbed a bite to eat and had a chat.

"Getting lots of pictures?" I asked.

"It's going very well, yes."

"Do me a favor. If you happen to see a sad looking girl on a black horse, I think she's number ninety-seven, get some pictures without asking her. I'm not even sure she's still here."

"She's with the Gold Sky Stables group. The horse's name is something Raven, isn't it?"

"I should have known you'd know everyone here," I laughed. "The horse is Rovin' Raven."

"I got some shots of her performing. I got the impression she wasn't trying very hard. I did ask if she wanted a portrait of her and her horse. She said no."

"Can you get something on the sly?"

"I can try."

I was making my way into the arena for my jumping class. For just a second I saw Brad with Kim Souder hanging on his arm. It so disoriented me I had to stop Hudson just inside the arena gate to refocus. I felt Hudson take a huge breath and blow it out. I smiled and did the same. Still, when we came out, I knew I hadn't done my best, and my body wasn't quite up to par. But I was hopeful that Hudson had covered for me. And he had. I was almost ashamed to accept the first place ribbon but figured that was a sure sign we were ready to move on to the next level.

The sun was true August hot and reflected from the water promising double whammy sun burns with or without sun screen. We did our best to stay coated with the lotion but we were in the water so much, I was sure we were going to suffer. We finally collapsed on our blanket under the umbrella ready to eat and relax.

"So what's with the sad girl on the black horse?"

"She's the daughter of my ex-boss and my friend Sara. I had tried to get Brooke some lessons at Phoenix but she didn't like the work part. She said Brad purchased a small farm so she could have a horse. Sara didn't say anything about that, but I haven't seen or talked to her recently. The relationship between Sara and Brad wasn't going well the last I talked to her. Sara was concerned about how Brooke was handling it. At the show, just as I was entering the jump arena, I saw Brad with this other woman. It totally shocked me. He had commented to me long ago that he'd never go with her."

"I thought you looked unfocused when you started your round."

"You don't miss much, do you?" I smiled at him.

"Not when the person matters to me."

I could feel my face grow warm with pleasure.

"So evidently he's changed his mind about this woman," he continued.

"I'm sure Brooke isn't happy about it. Were you able to get any shots of her and Raven?"

"No. I got a couple of her horse but I never saw her near the horse."

"I know you were busy. I really appreciate your efforts."

77

CHAPTER ELEVEN

Between all the sun and exercise, I slept like a log Sunday night. The alarm totally surprised me Monday morning. It took a second to realize it was now my first day of work at Stahlman, Stidd, and Austin. I knew it would be a much bigger challenge. I felt the excitement coursing through my body, and relief that I would soon have a regular pay check being deposited in the bank.

I still had time to hit the gym for my regular routine. I had already broken a sweat when Sara stepped on the treadmill next to me with a cheery "Good morning."

"Good morning, yourself. How's it going?"

"Okay."

"I saw Brooke at the horse show on Sunday. She didn't look very happy."

"No, she isn't. I haven't seen you to talk to you. Brad and I are definitely divorcing."

"Oh, Sara, I'm so sorry. Is it going to be civil?"

"Well, so far it has been. Brooke wanted to go with Brad because she thinks it's my fault. He said that was fine; one less child to pay support on. But when Brooke found out he was dating and planning to marry the Souder woman, the farm and horse he bought for her weren't good enough."

"She really looked sad. Unfortunately, she didn't look like she was trying very hard."

"I didn't know about the show or I would have been there. I guess she isn't speaking to me."

"I wish there was a way I could help Brooke. What do Marcus and Mariah say about the situation?"

"They think it's about Kim and Courtney so they think it's my fault also. Mariah rolled her eyes and said 'your relationship should be beyond that'. I didn't really share with them my need for some say in my own life. Heather is the only one that sees my side of it. The twins both say they'll stay at school to keep their distance. I'm really feeling guilty. Guess I should have waited until the kids were on their own."

"I think trying to get a job ten years from now would have been harder on you."

"You're right. It would have been. Speaking of…how's your job search coming?"

"I start at Stahlman, Stidd and Austin this morning."

"Here in Montaine?"

"Yep. They gave me more than Brad was paying me so I grabbed it."

"We need to go out to celebrate."

"Sounds good to me."

"Let's go back to Bubba's in Groveport Sunday night."

"You're on."

The atmosphere at Stahlman, Stidd and Austin was a complete turnabout from the last time I'd been there when they were so eager to hire me. There was no welcoming comments; no time to find the restroom. I asked Janice where my desk was located and she just shrugged her shoulders. I asked a few more people and finally had to ask a suit which turned out to be Mr. Austin. He scowled as he pointed me in the right direction.

My office had a door on each wall. On the other side of three of them was a lawyer. I was soon to learn the attorney's used those doors often, as did the paralegals which often clogged my escape door. I was glad for the experience I'd gotten at the Hartman office. These guys were going to make me earn that extra dollar right from the start. I was determined to help them see I was worth that extra dollar and more.

Marshall called when I got home just to say 'hi' and ask how my first day went.

"It was a challenge," I replied. "Once I settle in and know where everything is, it'll be fine."

"Want to get together, say Wednesday evening? We could see a movie and go out to eat."

"There's nothing showing that I'm dying to see, unless you have something picked out. We could even eat in. What sounds good to you?"

"Why don't we at least eat out. The diner has great chicken specials on Wednesday evenings. We could walk down and back; hit the video store on the way back."

"Alright."

"What are you doing this weekend?"

"There's a show in Damascus on Saturday. Sunday evening Sara and I are going to Bubba's in Groveport to celebrate my entrance back into employment."

"I have to show a couple houses Saturday morning but I'll try to catch up with you afterwards at the show."

"Drive careful."

I had more than enough points to move up another level in dressage and arena jumping despite being laid up for two months. I was going to participate in only two more shows and then focus on decreasing Hudson's conditioning, but also start working on higher levels in dressage and arena jumping. Arielle was working with Hudson and me. I was worried who I'd get for instruction after she left for college and asked her for a reference. She suggested Shelly or Brandi.

"Who's Brandi.

"She instructs the upper level adult students on Tuesday evenings in the saddle club arena after the kids leave, and the upper level school kids on Saturday mornings in the main arena. She has dark brown hair, brown eyes. She usually, but not always, goes to the shows with her students. I'll point her out to you this weekend."

"I think I know who you're talking about. So are you and Cavalier ready to leave for school?"

"Actually, Cavalier and Cherry Tart are both staying behind for Madison to use as schooling mounts. She's offered me Boudoir to use at school. Because of his talent and my experience, if we pull in lots of points for the school during the first year shows, I could get a scholarship for the following year."

"That's great, Arielle. I'm sure you'll have no trouble doing that. Do you think you'll come back to this area after you graduate?"

"Probably. Madison is looking at expanding Phoenix and wants me to come back as head instructor and trainer." Arielle had a grin on her face.

I had to smile with her. "Dream come true?"

"I can't believe it's happening, but Madison has always made good things happen."

Sunday afternoon Sara picked me up with the top down on her Mustang convertible. As I climbed in, she handed me a scarf. I pulled my hair back into a low ponytail, tied it with the scarf, which I then braided into the rest of the tail and knotted it at the loose end.

"I'm feeling wild and free," she said.

"Is there a specific reason? You look happy."

"We had our meeting with the lawyers Friday. I didn't realize I'd be so relieved. He'll let me have the house, pay off my car, child support for Heather, and alimony until I remarry. He gets the farm, custody of Brooke and gets to claim the twins on his taxes."

"Sounds pretty cut and dry."

"It's almost too good to be true."

"He won't pay off the house?"

"I don't think that's fair if he has to pay for college too. I can handle the house payment and expenses until I sell and downsize. Heather and I don't need that much room."

"I know a great real estate agent that will help you find just what you need," I grinned.

We ordered our honey/Bar-B-Q wings; talked of 'what ifs' and fantasy scenarios for our futures; swilled ice teas and watched the 'boots' start to arrive. We decided it had to be the atmosphere at Bubbas that compelled guys and gals alike to wear cowboy boots, and laughed at ourselves for conforming. We watched the line dances carefully, and when we thought we had the steps memorized, we got up to give it a go. We were just sitting down, damp from the exertion, laughing with delight when Marshall and Justin Hughes walked in.

Marshall gave me a wink as Justin gushed, "Sara, it's good to see you again. How've you been?"

"I've been fine, thank you."

"May I have a dance at some point this evening?"

"Sure."

"Great. Talk to you later."

"Enjoy yourself," whispered Marshall as he slid past, our bodies brushing against each other.

I felt the electrical charge down my spine as I watched him walk away. They found a table and Marshall sat with his back to us, blocking Justin's view.

Sara raised her eye brows. "What's with that?"

"I have no idea."

When we got up for another attempt at the line dance, the fellas did too, but afterwards went back to their table and worked on chowing on their meal. When a slow song came on, they both came and asked us to dance. In Marshall's arms, I said nothing. I was afraid anything I said might start a fight, as it would have with Josh. I didn't want to break the spell cast by the warmth of his arm around my waist. But when he asked the first question, I couldn't resist exploring the matter further.

"Having a good time?" he finally asked.

"Yes, but I'm a bit perplexed.

"About?"

"What you're doing."

"Dancing."

"I mean sitting across the room, and with your back to me."

"Justin really likes Sara. He's nagged me about her since that night we ran into you here. So when you said you were coming again, I thought it would be a good way to get them together, but I made him promise we weren't going to monopolize your time. I know this is girlfriend time and I don't want to ruin it for the two of you. I know Sara isn't actually free yet and may not want anyone in pursuit of her."

"How considerate of you."

All that week I marveled at Marshall's non-controlling behavior. How confident he must be in himself to give others such freedom. I had to laugh when I remembered I hadn't been likewise. I had glowered when the women with low necklines leaned over their table to chat and reveal. I had had to switch chairs so that my back was to them. Sara had laughed and I eventually had laughed as well, but the knot in my solar plexus was still there.

I was leaving the office each night totally exhausted. I hadn't even the energy to go to Phoenix. Madison called early Wednesday morning to ask if I was okay.

"This new job is quite a challenge. I may not get out there until Saturday morning. Do you have any students or stable hands that want to earn extra money? I'd appreciate someone giving Hudson a good grooming and lunge him."

"Will do," she assured me. "You won't be going with us to the show then?"

"No. I probably won't make the next one either."

"Oh, by the way, we have a new boarder that says she knows you."

"Who's that?"

"Angel Locke."

My mind went blank for a moment until I remembered Angel's maiden name was Locke."

"I can't believe it!"

"She said you'd be shocked," laughed Madison.

CHAPTER TWELVE

If I was going to allow myself five days to adjust to the job, I figured I'd better use the evenings in some productive way. I called each of my foster sisters for a chat.

Sidney said she was devastated that I was working for someone other than her husband but her voice wasn't screeching.

"We really need to get together for lunch," I urged.

"I'll drive to Montaine and meet you…where? When?"

"There's a Grandma's Diner across from the library on Main Street. How about next Wednesday evening?"

"Sounds good. See you then."

I called Dee Dee and got her answering machine. "Hey sis; just calling to say 'hi'. Hope your week is going good. I started a job here in Montaine. Feels safe to be working again. Take care. Talk to you later."

Hannah was next on the list.

"Jewel, I'm so glad you called. How's the job search going?"

"I started Monday. It's a bigger challenge as the firm has three lawyers instead of one. I'll definitely be earning my money."

"Congratulations. How's your knee?"

"My knee?"

"You kept rubbing it at the cookout."

I thought hard trying to remember rubbing my knee. Then I recalled the way she was watching me stroke the standard poodle's head. "I don't remember my knee hurting but I did want to ask you about the black poodle I was petting. Is it related to the one I used for a pillow in the album pictures? She looks exactly like the one that was at the cookout."

"I remember our Sophi. She seemed to be everyone's confidante. I remember telling her all my woes. But I don't remember seeing any poodle at the cookout."

"But I was petting her as you and I were talking. She even followed my car down the lane as I left. She sat at the end and watched me leave."

"Oh my gosh. Sophi did that the morning you left for college. She sat there all day waiting for you to return. We had to go bring her back to the house at supper time. She died maybe two years later. I remember there were some times she would lay on the porch with her front paws crossed, watching intently down the lane."

I was silent.

"Jewel?"

"Sounds a bit fantastical."

"Strange maybe, but I've heard some pretty strange things in my practice."

"Am I nuts?"

"I don't think so. You just have a spirit dog that was pleased to see you. You be sure to let me know if she's there the next time you go out to see Mom and Dad," laughed Hannah.

I had to calm down a bit before I could make my last phone call. I took a shower, made a cup of tea, got out the album and looked at the dog's picture. I had read a lot of stories about dogs appearing after their death to their owners. I felt blessed to have had the experience.

Just before crawling into bed, I dialed Angel's number. A gruff voice answered, "Hello?"

"Alex, this is Jewel. Is Angel there?"

"Nope. She split."

"Oh...I'm sorry."

"Want her new phone number?"

"If you have it; that would be great."

I called the number, which had a Creighton area code, and got an answering machine. "Angel, this is Jules. What's going on? Are you okay? I hear you're boarding a horse at Phoenix stables. That's a long haul from your area code. Give me a call."

When I got home from work the following evening, Angel's voice was on my machine.

"Jules, I thought I'd run into you at the stables by now. I'm assuming you'll be at the Drummond show on Saturday. I'll see you there, if not before."

There was no getting out of the show now. I had to go and compete. That meant I'd better get out to the stables and discuss it with Hudson, and let Madison know I'd changed my mind. I changed into breeches and boots, and headed for Phoenix. Hudson looked well groomed. There was a note on the cork board outside his stall saying Alyssa had groomed and lunged him half an hour on Tuesday and Wednesday. Hudson came on the run at the call of his name. I felt the excitement begin to charge up my body. He shoved his nose into my chest as if to ask where I'd been. I didn't usually allow such a breech of etiquette but decided it was my fault for neglecting him. I'd let it slide just this once.

We were soon on the cross country course. It took all I had to hold him in check. He wanted to explode over the jumps. I was afraid if I let him out between jumps he wouldn't check before flying over them. I made a mental note that we needed to work on calmness on the course.

He still had a lot of energy when we got back so we worked over the arena jumps and then went through the dressage maneuvers. After bathing him, I covered him with his cooler to keep him somewhat clean, and let him settle into his grain. I was headed to Shelly's office to leave Alyssa's pay with her when Angel came down from the judges' box.

"That was pretty impressive," she said.

"Angel!" I threw my arms around her in a hug. "Why didn't you let me know you were here?"

"I wanted to watch before you knew. You are a marvelous horsewoman."

"Thanks. Where's your horse?"

"Down at the end."

"Are you going to compete?"

"Just in cross country. I'm easing myself down from the reckless gradually," she said with a wry grin.

I had done an about face to walk to the stall where Angel's horse was munching hay. He was big but looked rather tame.

"And this is…?"

"Lord Baruk. He's a Thoroughbred/Arab cross."

"He doesn't look your type, Angel."

"Wait 'til you see him in action. Are you doing cross country yet?"

"Practicing but not competing. Next year. We're still in dressage and arena jumping. Hudson is ready. I'm the one still learning."

Alyssa was walking a horse toward us for a stall close by. I held out my hand, palm down, to pass the folded bills to her. She smiled and said "Thanks."

"Do you have time for a cup of coffee or something?" asked Angel.

"Sure. We can get one here in the break room. I don't think there's any place near where you or I wouldn't have to go out of our way." I put a dollar in the can to help with buying the coffee and poured two cups. "So, Alex said you split. He seemed awfully calm about it."

"He thinks I'll be back."

"Will you?"

"Not soon. Maybe not ever. I'm impressed with how you've rediscovered yourself. I think I'd like to find me, also."

"I couldn't have done it without your help, Angel."

She put her arm around my shoulder and squeezed. "What are friends for?"

It wasn't until I was almost home that I realized I was tired. I had felt so energized while at the stables with CastleontheHudson. I felt bad that earlier in the week I had thought I was too tired to work with him. He was what I needed all along. I was even glad I

87

Rae D'Arcy

still had one or two shows left to compete in before the season would be over.

I had two messages on my answering machine when I got home. I called Hannah first. "What's up, Sis?"

"Jules, I hope you don't mind but I tracked down Fisher for you."

For a moment I couldn't get my mouth to work. "Why would I want you to do that?" I finally asked.

""I guess I thought he was an important part of your past that you should revisit."

"Are you saying that as a sister or as a psychiatrist?"

"Both. Look, just take his address and phone number and think about it."

"What if he doesn't want to talk to me?"

"He does. I asked him."

"So now if I don't contact him I'll disappoint him all over again."

"I warned him you may not."

"And he said what?"

"Whatever."

The paper with Fisher's address and phone number felt hot in my hand as I returned Marshall's call. My face burned. I felt just thinking of contacting Fisher made me unfaithful to Marshall.

"How'd the first couple days go on the new job?" he asked.

"Rough, but I'm adjusting. I was so tired the first couple nights I didn't even go to Phoenix. I forced myself to go tonight and was so charged. I didn't realize I was tired until on the way home."

"Hudson really is the source of your horse power, isn't he?"

"He is indeed. I thought I was done competing for the year but now I think I want to do those last two shows."

"Wow. He charged you that much."

"Well, actually a friend from my past is stabling a horse at Phoenix now and is competing this weekend so I decided to do those last two shows mostly to go see her take on the cross country course and show her what Hudson and I can do."

"What's her name? I'll make sure I get pictures."

"Angel Locke. Her horse's name is Lord Baruk."

"And is Hudson ready?"

"He is so ready. And what have you been up to?"

"They have a new fella joining the saddle club. I told Madison I'd mentor the next one they got. This little guy is only ten so it's going to be a long term commitment. I actually called to let you know it would be occupying a night a week for a long while."

"I think that's great. Is this a guy thing or can I join you on some outings?"

"Sometimes it's a guy thing but an occasional outing with the fairer sex would be okay. Why don't you mentor one of the girls?"

"I don't think I'm cut out for it. I tried to encourage Sara's daughter, Brooke, and failed miserably. Besides, I'm not sure I'll have the energy to do double duty at the stables."

"You should give it another try. You don't have to be at the saddle club with them unless you want to. The instructors take care of that. Mostly it's just a night a week just hanging out."

"Well, I'll think about it. Let me get more settled in my job and then we'll see."

"The saddle club is having a play day Sunday afternoon. My little guy, Corey, is participating. I want to be there for him so how about dinner out Monday night?"

"Sounds great. Casual or formal?"

"Casual okay with you? Say, Bubba's?"

"It's a date. See you this Saturday at the show."

I dialed Fisher's number next before I chickened out. My face flamed red. How could I just make plans with the man I loved and then call another?

"Hello," answered a tenor voice.

I knew deep in my solar plexus who this was and still I said, "Hello, this is Jewel Fitzgerald. I'm calling for Fisher Price."

"Hello Jewel. This is Fisher. It's been a long time."

"I...I really don't know what to say, Fisher. I guess I hurt you. I don't remember, but someone said I didn't say good-bye to you and you were my boyfriend."

"That's their interpretation of it. We did say good-bye in our own ways. We were more friends but pretty close. We basically helped each other to accept who we were, and how to play the cards life had dealt us. Would you care to get together to catch up on our lives?"

"Do you have a significant other?" At first I wondered why I had put it like that, and a second later remembered that the cards of life he had been dealt was being gay.

"No. There's a place in Groveport called Daphne's. Sunday afternoon, about two?"

"That's about a block before Bubba's isn't it?" I asked not expecting or waiting for an answer. "I'll be there."

I knew Marshall would be with Corey. I had no fear of running into him in Groveport. Sunday was perfect for meeting with Fisher.

CHAPTER THIRTEEN

The temperatures dropped Friday night to give us a cool weekend. It made competing more pleasant on Saturday and the warmth and coziness of Daphne's more enjoyable on Sunday.

The main lunch rush was thinning out so I sat at a table and ordered a coffee while looking the place over, and keeping one eye focused on the entrance. It was a cute place with checkered table clothes. The bouquets of real flowers on the table were surprisingly fragrant, and looked fresher than the waitresses who had just worked the lunch hour. They were still hustling to get the dining area tidied before the late eaters came in.

I sensed, more than saw, the thin angular man coming toward me. I was about to look his way when I locked eyes with Sara as she was getting up from a table across the room. The man who took her elbow was Justin Hughes. I saw her face turn pink as I felt mine doing the same.

"Jules?"

I had to turn my attention to Fisher. I forced a smile. I was all too aware of what this rendezvous must look like to the couple coming toward us. I was desperately trying to think of an explanation to give Sara and Justin when she leaned down and whispered, "Busted. Both of us. Talk to you at the gym in the morning."

I forced a laugh. Sara would be no problem but would Justin call Marshall? Now what would I do? As they were going out the door,

I thought I should have just introduced Fisher as a friend from my childhood.

Fisher had taken a seat and was watching me watch my friend's exiting back. "I take it you didn't expect to see anyone you knew here."

"No, I didn't." I looked at Fisher. "And the guy I date is busy right now so I thought it was safe to meet with you."

He laughed coarsely. "Will she tell?"

"Not Sara but I don't know about Justin."

"Best to be up front."

"I should have been up front to begin with but I wasn't sure how he'd react. My ex would have made a big deal about it and told me I couldn't come."

"And this new guy is like that?"

"Not that I can see. But this issue has never come up before."

"You should have trusted him until he gave you reason not to."

"What's that saying about hindsight? Twenty/twenty?"

"Yep."

I took a deep breath to shift emotional gears. "Well, Fisher, what do you do for a living?"

"I'm in juvenile crime."

"Wow. I'm impressed." I paused looking him over. He had a hooked nose. It might have been broken. He had black hair, dark eyes, high cheekbones. Possible Indian background, I wondered? Narrow shoulders, long fingers. "You'll have to forgive me, Fisher. I don't remember much. What was our relationship like?"

"We were awesome friends."

"So I just walked away and forgot you?"

"No. We said our good-byes. I had hoped you'd keep in touch but you had a way of focusing on the task at hand that excluded all else. It was outstanding that we were friends while we were in high school. So you had made progress and I had hoped it was enough that would enable you to keep me in mind. But when you didn't, I figured you were just overwhelmed with the demands of college."

"Progress from what?"

"Totally withdrawn from the outer world. Totally focused on your studies, or your horse, or swimming, or ball. It was like you lost yourself in them. You became a part of your horse, a part of the water, even a part of history, numbers, even grammar and the stories you created."

"What was it about you that helped me get to the place where I could have you as a friend and still focus on the other things enough to do well?"

"Probably because I'm gay and you didn't need to worry about second guessing me."

"Gosh, did we discuss it?"

"A lot. I was so scared. It was such a relief to be able to just be me. Neither one of us was interested in being sexual. We talked about so many things. Do you still write?"

"Did I write?"

"Great stuff. I still have the copies of the stories."

"Could I read them?"

"Sure. But that means we'll have to get together again." His brow furrowed, his eyes turned darker. I could see he doubted I'd say yes.

I reached across the table and touched his hand. "Yes. Shall we meet here next Sunday?"

He smiled and told me more about his life before we parted. He left a hefty tip just because we monopolized the table while nursing coffees and a single piece of pie.

I called Marshall that evening. "Hey, how'd the play day go?"

"Not too good. Corey expected to be able to do the harder events and was really upset when he couldn't. He's got some real anger issues."

"And who takes care of those?"

"We'll all try to help him. John Smith has the unpleasant task of limiting his time with his mount if he hurts it...and he did. He gets to muck stalls but no riding for a week. I'll take him on some kind of outing so he isn't totally shut out. It can't hurt too bad or they get discouraged and quit."

"Poor fella."

"They usually learn pretty fast to control it. What did you do?"

My face flushed as I tried to keep my voice from quavering and said, "Went to Groveport to meet up with an old friend. I didn't remember him while Hannah talked about him but after I met him, it all came back."

"An old boyfriend? I'm jealous."

"Not a boyfriend. He's gay which is why I felt so safe with him back then. And you have no need to feel jealous. No one could take your place."

"Is that right?"

My face deepened another shade of red with embarrassment that I had so carelessly made such a bold statement. What if Marshall didn't feel the same about me?

"We're going to meet again next Sunday. He said I used to write stories. I don't remember that. But he kept copies and is going to let me read them."

"Maybe I should come along, just in case."

"I would love for you to meet him. Then again," I said with a chuckle, "maybe I'll be the jealous one."

Sara was already on the treadmill by the time I got to the gym Monday morning. We both burst into laughter.

"What a bust. We both thought we could be sneaky. So who was the little bird man?"

"An old friend from my past; Fisher. He's gay so don't get excited. So you're seeing Justin?"

"Now and again. I guess I didn't want it widely known until I'm more sure about if and where it's going. He upset me with his attitude when he saw you with Fisher. He thought you were cheating on Marshall. I told him it was none of his business. He said Marshall was his friend and needed to know. So have you spoken with Marshall?"

"Last night."

"Is he okay with it?"

"I think so. I was determined to be truthful so I just said it all in one breath and ended on a humorous note. Fisher seems to be very angry. I want to be his friend again."

"Why?"

"He confided a lot to me. I feel bad for him."

"Watch it sweety. He'll pick up on that sympathy and start stalking you."

"Oh, don't say that. It scares me, but I owe him."

"You owe him nothing."

"He was a friend when I needed one."

"You were his friend too. And then you went your separate ways."

"I can see your point, but I think he could use a friend now too. I've been so blessed with friends. I'd like to pass some on."

We moved on to another type of machine to work our abs.

"What kind of work does he do?" grunted Sara.

"He's in juvenile crime," I grunted back.

Sara's mouth dropped. "I can picture big teen age boys knocking him down and stomping all over him."

I laughed. "No, he told me a stint in the Marines, and as a policeman with a black belt has made him a trained killer. I'm sure he can hold his own."

"All the more reason not to take him home with you."

Wednesday came. Although usually my downtime night, I was agitated and felt some time with Hudson would calm me. I was dressed to go to the stables when I remembered my dinner with Sidney. I wouldn't have time to ride but I could at least groom Hudson. He had done wonderful at the show in both classes. I worked him hard Monday and Tuesday evenings so I guessed a night off wouldn't hurt him.

I was just about to put Hudson in his stall after grooming and a good massage, which Shelly had shown me how to do, when a student brought Cavalier into the grooming bay. It hit me then that Arielle had left for college. I had been so wrapped up in my own life, I hadn't noticed her absence. I remembered telling her to send me her address once she got settled but she was probably busy. I gave Hudson a carrot and headed for Shelly's office.

"Shelly, has anyone heard from Arielle?"

"She called a couple days ago and gave her address and phone number for anyone that wants it."

"Oh good. I certainly do."

I was determined to return the friendship of the many people who had befriended me. As I raced through the rain to my car, I decided to stop at the Pizza Shop and get Arielle a gift certificate. It was a national chain. Surely they'd have one near the Erie College.

As I entered Grandma's I was aware of the wet horse aroma I was exuding. Sidney sat at a booth. She smiled and waved as I made my way to her.

"Sidney, I'm so sorry I smell like wet horse. If you want we can do this another time, or I can dash home for a shower. I live close by. Shouldn't take more than a half hour."

"No, no. I've been looking forward to this for the past six days. I won't let you get away." She closed her eyes and inhaled deeply. "Besides, I love the smell of horse. I miss it so much."

"Why don't you get one. Dad said it would be nice to have a horse in the barn again."

"Oh, I don't think Bob would let me."

"But he said…"

"To get you to work for him. You refused his offer."

"So he's punishing you."

"I wouldn't call it that."

"I would." I grinned mischievously. "Tell him it'll firm your thighs and backside."

She laughed. "Good try but I don't think it'll work. He'll say that's why he gave me the gym membership."

"As hard as you work to please him, I think you deserve some happiness."

Sidney's eyes filled with tears. "Thanks. I needed to hear that. Thanks for having dinner with me."

"Sidney, don't you have other friends you go out with?"

"I used to, but Bob went to bed with all of them. I just couldn't like them after that."

"All of them?" I asked wide eyed and drop jawed.

"All except you."

CHAPTER FOURTEEN

Thursday on the way to Phoenix, I got a pizza gift card for Arielle. At the stables I put a note on the message board in the break room asking for riding time on someone's horse for Sidney. After riding, I wrote Arielle a letter and enclosed the pizza gift certificate. I'd post it on the way to the gym in the morning. Then I called Sara.

"Hey, just called to say hi and ask how Brooke is doing?"

"Still brooding. I hear she's on the verge of losing her horse because she doesn't take very good care of it. The stables she was riding for won't let her compete in their colors because her attitude is so poor."

"Do you think Brad would mind if I trailer Hudson over there to ride with Brooke?"

"They have two horses. Why not just ride Chelsea's?"

"They got one for Chelsea?"

"Yeah, but she's off to college so Brooke has to care for both and she isn't happy about that."

"Do you think Brad would mind?"

"No. He'll accept any help he can get with the child. Are you sure you want to spend time with her?"

"At this point, yes. I'm determined to try harder."

"Good luck. I'll appreciate it if you can get through to her."

I called Brad's house. Kim answered. "Kim, this is Jules Fitzgerald. Is Brad there?"

"How do you know Brad?" she asked suspiciously.

"I used to work for him."

"He doesn't need any more help."

"I'm not calling about a job."

"Then what do you want?"

"May I speak to Brad, please." I could hear him in the background asking who it was and then with hand over the transmitter, Kim saying my name.

"Jules, this is Brad. How are you?"

"Very well, thank you. I was calling to see if you'd mind if I came to ride with Brooke. I could trailer my horse out there but Sara said you got Chelsea a horse. I could ride it and keep it somewhat exercised for her. Do you think Brooke would mind my company?"

He laughed. "I'll guarantee she'll act like she's just putting up with you but beneath the show, I'll bet she'll be glad for the company."

"Is she there? Shall I ask her first?"

"Kim, call Brooke from her room will you? So Jules, how's the job? I hear Stahlman, Stidd and Austin are a rough bunch to work for."

"It is a challenge."

"Have they started demanding you work over to help the paralegals yet?"

I gulped. "No. Is that a habit with them?"

"That's what I've heard."

"I guess that gives me something to look forward to."

Brad laughed and then said, "Here's Brooke."

"Hello?"

"Brooke, this is Jules. I was wondering if you'd like a riding buddy one night a week while Chelsea is away. I can help groom and keep her horse exercised for her."

"Yeah, I guess."

"Okay. Would Thursday evening about five thirty be okay?"

"I think so."

"Alright. See you then."

"Sure."

I had a new attitude when I got to work the next morning. It was called dread. Would they, indeed, expect me to start staying over later? I was on salary so it wouldn't be overtime. There had already been a few nights I had left a half hour late, and even worked through lunch on several occasions to get out by five. I knew I wasn't going to be a happy camper if it got worse. I was trying to convince myself not to worry until I had something to worry about.

"So are you going with me?"

"You mean to have lunch with Fisher?"

"Yes."

"Do you really want me to?"

"Yes. I want you to know who my friends are. I know you can't predict who you'll like and won't like but I hope you can at least tolerate him. Everyone needs friends."

"What makes you think he doesn't have friends?"

"I was referring to me. I feel the need to reconnect with these people from my past. I'm amazed at the sense of family they've given me. I'm so glad I've found them. I feel more complete. And if I can add something to their lives, I want to."

"You're a kind soul, aren't you?"

"I don't think I was before I came to Montaine but the kindness from my new and old friends has rubbed off onto me."

I had to admit to myself, I was worried about how Fisher would react to my bringing Marshall. He had a wide grin when he first saw me. When I introduced Marshall as my friend, something flickered in his eyes but his handshake with Marshall was firm. I liked that.

He handed me a business-paper box. "Don't try reading them all now. Let's just visit. You can make copies if you want but I'd really like to have these back. Even though they are yours, you did give them to me."

"No problem."

We ordered our meals and Fisher told us about his job. I could tell Marshall was impressed. Marshall told Fisher about the saddle club and Fisher said it was a good idea to help them and keep his work load lighter. I promised to call him for another lunch date after I had read the stories. On the way home, we stopped to rent a movie and took it to my place. My answering machine was blinking.

"Jules, this is Josie. I'm leasing the horse in stall ten while Karen is at college. Karen said as long as Madison thought your friend was experienced enough, she could ride Castle Guard. If she wanted to ride regularly, maybe she could help a little with the lease expense? Let me know."

"What is that all about?"

"Sidney misses riding and hasn't any friends. I thought this would be a good way to get her out a bit. I'll introduce her to Angel and Sara. Maybe we can start a girls' night out once a month or so."

Marshall smiled as he put the DVD in the machine. "Let me know how it works out."

Angel and I trail rode together Tuesday evening. When I got home, I called Sidney.

"Hey, would you like to go horseback riding?"

"I'd love to. Where?"

"At the stables where I board Hudson. All you have to do is go out and demonstrate your experience. Then you can ride as often as you like if you help a little with the lease cost."

"Oh, that would be so wonderful."

"Can you come out Sunday afternoon for the test drive?"

"No. That's the only day I have with Bob. I could Friday morning."

"Let me give you the number and directions. Madison or Shelly will be the ones to determine if your skill is sufficient. With the show experience you had growing up; I doubt you'll have any trouble. Let me know how it goes."

Thursday evening I barely made it to Brad's farm by five thirty. We had to walk out into the pasture to get the horses. They didn't run from us but didn't come to our call, either.

"So who's this fella?"

"Chelsea calls him Fred."

"Hello Fred. You look like you could use a bath."

I saw Brooke's cheeks flush. "Maybe after we ride we can bathe them."

"Okay."

It took awhile to get Fred presentable. Rovin' Raven wasn't in much better shape. We finally mounted up and rode through the fields. The evening sun was still warm and cast an orange sheen over the countryside. We walked for the most part. Afterward, I tried to keep the conversation going to make bathing the horses fun. I scrubbed the feed pans and water buckets not mentioning their crusty condition or lecturing on how they should be kept clean.

"Well, I'll see you next Thursday? Oh, when does school start?"

"Monday."

"Wow. The summer went quick didn't it?"

"Yeah."

"Are you sure Thursdays will still be okay for riding?"

"It should be."

"Okay then; see you Thursday."

I couldn't believe how Brooke's one word answers exhausted me. It was hard trying to carry the conversation. I was sure I wasn't going to do anything strenuous once I got home. So I got out the stories I had written long ago. I was shocked at the cruelty they contained but also at the sensitivity and skill with which they were written. Tears streamed down my face and the dry humor made me laugh. How could I not remember writing these tales of woe?

After reading three manuscripts, I took a spiral note book out on the balcony with a cup of tea. It was cooling off but I knew my layered clothing would keep me warm. As the sun sank beneath the horizon, I sat, pen in hand, blankness in mind, until I had to go in for a candle. I sat back and watched the flame flicker. Just start writing anything, I said to myself. The hand began to move: ' As the sky turned indigo around her, the candle's flame danced the mambo and frogs sang from a distant pond out in the pasture....'

CHAPTER FIFTEEN

Summer had not yet exited before the talk around Phoenix was about the fall trail ride.

"It's a lot of fun. You should come, Sidney."

"No. I'm really enjoying riding. I don't want to do anything to rock the boat and cause Bob to deny me that pleasure. Besides, I heard Josie pointedly saying she'd be attending on Castle Guard. She does have first dibs on him."

"He's really getting muscled up with both you and Josie riding him."

"He is looking sharp, isn't he?"

Sidney leaned forward to look across Hudson's neck at Angel. "Will you be going Angel?"

"Oh yeah. I hear it's the talk of the equine set."

The horses were starting to prance as we neared the place we usually let them canter or gallop.

"Ready to turn 'em loose ladies?" asked Angel.

I was calming Hudson with a still seat and a light hold on the reins. "I'm going to make Hudson walk as you take off."

"You're going to make him hate you."

"It's called training, Angel."

"Oh pooh. Come on, Sidney, let's go."

Lord Baruk and Castle Guard bolted forward. It took only a squeeze and a slight pull on the reins to remind Hudson to remain at a walk although his head was high, ears pricked, liquid eyes watching the other horses disappear behind the trees. The thundering hoofs were fading in the distance and then I cued Hudson for a canter. He made no effort to charge ahead. He simply gave what I asked. Even when the other horses returned sweaty and blowing, Hudson remained calm and steady. I patted him on his neck and told him what a good boy he was. I wanted to reward him with a good run but decided to maintain the lesson. Even as the other horses were heading for the barn, we kept toward the fields.

The sun was glowing gold as it began to near the horizon. I stopped Hudson and sat still watching the molten colors spread along the rim of the earth. I felt a calm wash over me. I knew I had needed some quiet time.

Life had felt crowded since Sidney, Angel, Brooke and I had become riding buddies. Marshall and I still went out once or twice a week and I was rediscovering writing. I had let Marshall read the stories I had written so long ago. He was adamant that I had a talent that I should attempt to reactivate. As I met the pen at the paper to play, I was amazed at what flowed from the tip of the pen onto the blank lines like rain finding a dry creek bed to channel its flow.

I was disappointed that Brooke wasn't making more of an effort in caring for Raven and Fred, but I was determined to be patient. Still, it seemed they only got groomed when I was there. The stalls were seldom clean. Water buckets had old water in them and feed pans were getting crusty. I wondered, if they didn't have access to the pasture, would they be starving? I was starting to get angry for the horses' sakes.

Thursday morning, I got a call from Dee Dee. "How about lunch?" she asked.

"I usually work through lunch so I can get out on time," I apologized.

"Well, dinner then."

"I'd love to. I'll already be half way to your place in Augusta. I can come the rest of the way and meet you between seven and seven thirty."

"Sounds good. There's a place just inside the town limits called Gossip Alley. See you there."

I lost my temper with Brooke that evening. As usual the horses needed extensive grooming and the feed and water containers needed scrubbed. "You know Brooke, if you'd have this stuff done, we could spend more time riding."

"I don't care. I want Dad to sell the horses. It's too much work."

"Brooke, Raven could be your best friend. I get the impression you need one."

"No, I don't. I have a boyfriend."

"Boyfriends aren't usually very good friends." I turned to look at her. She was sitting on a step stool playing with the wet bristles of a scrub brush, the dirty feed pan still dirty. "Brooke!"

She jumped.

"Scrub. I have someplace else I have to be in a bit."

She threw the brush down and stomped out. "Then go!"

I finished grooming and scrubbing the pans and buckets, fed the horses and left. So I had failed a second time with her. I was angry at myself but at Brooke also. There were so many kids who would die for a horse of their own. The kids that had it handed to them sure didn't seem to appreciate it. The horses certainly deserved better care.

I began trying to figure out how I could help the horses. I had no doubt Brooke was serious about convincing her father to sell them. I liked both horses. Fred was calm and Raven's talent was definitely not being utilized. I could almost see him in my mind's eye blossoming under the right tutelage.

I had just taken a seat in the Gossip Alley foyer with all dark paneling and faux wood when Dee Dee walked in. When she saw me, she smiled and said, "Darn, I thought I was going to get a couple drinks before you showed."

"My previous engagement was cut short. We can order drinks with our meals, can't we?"

"Sure. Have something for me?" she asked eyeing my manila envelope.

"Fisher showed me some of my writing from high school. I wanted your opinion of them."

"They're great."

"Excuse me?"

"I've already seen them and they're great."

"I barely remember them. How could you have seen them already?"

"They were creative writing assignments of yours in Mrs. Prusser's class. Unfortunately, I was naïve and thought I could pass them off as mine when I got to her class," she laughed. "They were so awesome. I wanted to be able to write like that. For my first assignment I took the one titled Green Backed Chair and turned it in as my own. When Mrs. Prusser asked me to stay after class the next day, I was sure I was going to be praised for my talent. Instead, I was given a kindly lecture on plagiarism and a second chance to write my own story. A couple days later, I was again asked to stay. She said she could see how I was trying to imitate your style and it was coming out stilted. She gave me yet another chance. A couple days after that, another summons. She said, at last she could hear my voice and see my own style. She encouraged me to be me, not you, and to develop my own considerable talent."

"You wanted my talent?"

"And Mrs. Prusser was impressed enough with your work to remember your stories years after you had moved on and I tried to steal your work."

"Would you read a story I just wrote over the past week and tell me honestly what you think? It's the top one." I handed her the manila envelope.

"Sure. Now let me tell you what a difference you've made in Sidney's life."

A thank- you note arrived from Arielle saying it was her favorite pizza, classes were easy, Flash was impressing everyone, and their first school show would be in October. I had to stop and think. I thought she had taken Boudoir, not Flash. I'd have to ask Shelly about it. I'd seen her ride in many shows but I marked my calendar hoping to make the trip to watch her perform as a show of support.

Sunday evening Marshall came by. Lying on the couch, he looked tired.

"Are you okay?"

"Yeah, just tired and a bit frustrated."

"What's happening?"

"I've been working with this couple for over two years trying to find them a home. I'll bet I've shown them at least one a month meeting the specifications they gave me. But they always find something wrong with it. I've never gotten fed up with anyone before, but I think they've won the award."

"Maybe they aren't seriously in the market. Maybe it's just a source of entertainment or a way to think positive; to look and daydream, not realizing your time is valuable and they're a drain on you and your vehicle."

Marshall reached for my upper arm and pulled me over the back of the couch onto his lap. With a hand on either side of my face he pulled me forward into a gentle kiss.

"You are so patient, so wise."

"Not really. I totally lost it and failed again with Brooke."

"What happened?"

"She does nothing to care for those horses. I'm actually scared for the poor things. She walked out of the barn leaving me to finish the chores and not riding. I'm not even sure I should go next Thursday."

"We need something to cheer us up."

"I have salmon steaks. Can you stay for dinner?" I swung off his lap and headed for the kitchen.

"Thought you'd never ask."

"Hey, Arielle has her first school show October tenth. I want to go to support her. Want to go along?"

"Sure. She'll appreciate that. Wait, that date sounds familiar. Oh man, that's the trail ride."

"You help out every year don't you?"

"Yes. Do you think we'd get back in time?"

"I don't know what time her class is. Well, that's okay. Maybe you can catch a later show."

"You're not going to go to the trail ride?"

"I really think it's important to support Arielle and our friendship. I can go to the spring trail ride."

I felt Marshall's body heat warm my back as he gently pulled my hair away from my neck and kissed just beneath my ear. "What can I do to help?" he whispered.

Goose bumps rose on my arms. "I need the salad and lemon juice from the fridge."

CHAPTER SIXTEEN

Hudson and I stood watching the sun set in a clear western sky. The temperature was dropping faster than the sun making its way beneath the horizon. I was sorry I hadn't worn a jacket. Angel and Sidney had long since headed for the barn. When I started shivering, I turned Hudson's head homeward.

"Hud, I feel like all heck is about to break loose." His ears swiveled back as though wanting to hear more. "I don't know why I'm feeling this way. I'm worried about Brooke. What should I do? Quit going over there?"

I knew that's what I wanted someone to tell me; 'you are released from that chore'. But as dusk deepened around us I had a mental picture of me smiling at Brooke's sullen face and cheerfully doing her chores. Tears began to run down her face. I gave her a hug and suggested a ride. That seemed to be my answer. Even though it wasn't the one I wanted, it had a feeling of rightness to it and I knew that that would be my course…at least for awhile longer. Still, the knot in my stomach remained.

The dark square barn windows illuminated when someone turned on the lights. "Almost there Hudson. You're such a good boy." I patted his neck.

I was leading Hudson toward the grooming bays as Cindy Ley was leading Deek out. She stopped and Hudson put his muzzle against her cheek.

"He says he told you to help that girl."

I was speechless as Cindy and Deek continued on their way. By the time I found my voice she was too far away to yell, 'thank you.'

"Oh, Hudson, how awesome if you're trying to communicate with me." I leaned my head against his neck. "I am so blessed to have you."

There was a folded note stuck to the cork board outside Hudson's stall. It was signed "Sidney" and simply asked , "Are you mad at me?"

I called her as soon as I got home. "Sidney, no I am not mad at you."

"Why don't you ride with Angel and me anymore?"

"I do but I also need to bring Hud down from his show level of conditioning gradually so he doesn't cramp up this winter. And it's good training for him."

"Well, Angel says you're being a snob."

"And you say...?"

"I think you need some time alone."

"There is some truth to that. With everyone I'm trying to ride with, I have felt a bit crowded, but I'm not trying to be a snob. I just need a bit more space than most people."

"Yeah, you always did. Hey, Mom and Dad want you out for dinner."

"I'd love to. When?"

"Next Sunday, the eighth."

"I can make that but the fifteenth would be better."

"I think they're leaving for Florida and a cruise on the fourteenth."

"The eighth it is then. Can I bring a friend?"

Thursday I forced a smile on my face as I parked my car and headed for the barn at Brad's. I could see the horses out in the field; heads up, listening. They seemed to be wondering if I would call them. I decided to scrub the pans and buckets first.

Dusk was coming earlier every evening. I switched on the barn lights and went into the stalls for the feed pans and took them to the feed room. As I came back out to get the water buckets, I saw Brooke and a much older boy sitting on a bale of hay outside a stall. They hadn't been there before. I felt my face stiffen.

"Hello, Brooke. Are we going to ride?"

Looking down, she kicked some loose hay with her foot. "I don't know if I want to."

"Why don't you call the horses and start grooming?"

"I don't think so. Why don't we skip it. I'll scrub the pans. You can go. Have a night off."

I ignored her comment. "Are you going to introduce me to your friend?"

"Greg."

"Hello Greg."

He mumbled a greeting.

I scrubbed. I filled with water. I called the horses and groomed. I gave them their grain and then I turned them back out and rewashed the feed pans. Greg had made no move to leave. I had a bad feeling about leaving the two alone. I sat on a bale of hay nearby.

"So how's school going Brooke?"

"Okay."

"What grade are you in Greg?"

"I'm a junior."

"In sports?"

"Quarterback."

"Ah, a jock. Going to college?"

"Sure."

"Good for you. What field?"

"Football," he sneered.

"Of course. What about you Brooke?"

"I've got plenty of time to think about it."

I looked Greg hard in the eyes as I answered, "Yes, you are pretty young to be thinking grown up thoughts."

Greg scowled. "Brooke, I've got homework to do. I'll see you at the game tomorrow night."

Brooke watched him go with such longing in her eyes I almost cried. Just a child wanting someone to hold her and tell her everything would be all right. She didn't yet realize Greg's words wouldn't have the same meaning she attributed to them. I felt a call to Brad and Kim was in order.

Things were getting stressful at work. It seemed the paralegals were starting to increase the help they were asking of me. Brad's words rang in my ears about being asked to stay over to help them. If I had time, I'd do the research they asked but I made sure to let them know when I didn't have time or couldn't complete the task.

One rainy evening as Hudson and I finished a few jumps in the arena, I worried what I'd say when the demand came to stay and help. "Sorry, I have plans," was the immediate reply that came to mind.

Then I'll be jobless again, I moaned inwardly.

Not for long, a voice inside my head countered.

Cindy rode by on Deek.

"Cindy, wait." They stopped and I moved Hudson closer. "May I ask what Hudson is saying?"

"You know."

"I think I do, but what if I'm wrong?"

"You aren't."

"But how…why has he started communicating with me?"

"Because you're listening to him." She and Deek went on their way.

"Okay big boy. I'm going to rely on you. I'm going to trust you to give me horse power.

The next time Marshall and I went out, I asked him what he thought of Cindy's ability to communicate with the horses.

"I remember once when she first started riding at Phoenix; she was six or seven; she claimed one of the newer boarding horses was lost and wanted to go home. She even let him out of the stall. It turned out he had been stolen. I never doubted her ability again."

"Do you like kids?"

"As long as they go home at the end of the day."

I gulped. This was going to be our first major issues conversation.

"I suppose you want kids?" he countered.

I could hear the worry in his voice and saw it in his eyes. "To tell you the truth, I've never thought about having them. They're so easily hurt. I don't want to be responsible for doing that to a child."

"Probably because you were hurt in the extreme. My reasons are more selfish. I've never been married. I'm thirty-seven years old. Seems a bit late to start such a major project. I don't want to be dealing with a sixteen year old when I'm almost sixty years old."

"Why haven't you married?"

"I just had the feeling that instead of being concerned about growing, the women were all on the hunt for a caretaker. And I wonder what that says about me? Why was I dating those types of women? Maybe I had a commitment problem and felt like I was being cornered."

I took a deep breath. "Speaking of cornering you, Mom and Dad have invited me to dinner before they leave on a cruise. I asked if I could bring a friend. Would you like to go?"

He smiled. "Yes, I would."

I was pulling into Brad's place and realized the red mustang parked by the barn was Greg's, not Kim's. There were no lights on in the house or the barn. I felt my stomach knot up. I parked my own car and, without looking for the horses, hurried toward the barn through the light rain that had been falling all day. Just as I reached the door, Greg came barreling out hunched over as though running a play. He hit me full force and I flew backward hitting the ground hard. My head whipped back and hit the muddy ground with a thwack. Stars circled on impact. I heard his car start up. He gunned it, spewing gravel as he peeled down the lane.

I don't know how long I laid there before the darkness in my mind abated and I opened my eyes to a purple sky and rain drops pelting me. My head hurt. As I got up the horses whickered from the gate. I went inside turning on the lights as I passed the switch.

"Brooke?"

There was no answer but I thought I heard a noise in the feed room. I scurried as gently as I could, still holding my throbbing head, wiping my muddy hands on my pants; feeling the wet through the backside of my clothes. Brooke was sitting on a bale of straw, some of which was in her tangled hair and on her mussed clothes. Her eyes and nose were red and running.

"Brooke, are you all right?"

She only sniffed. The smell of dust made me want to sneeze. I pinched my nose while I waited a second for Brooke to answer.

"Brooke, did he hurt you? Answer me or I'll call the police."

"You can't. I said yes. The police can't touch him."

"You said y..." As realization dawned in my aching head, I had flashbacks of my own ordeal; felt the physical pain and emotional fear as I struggled with what to do for Brooke. I went to her and put my arms around her. "Sweetie, I think I should call your mom."

"Liz said it was great." A huge sob exploded from her chest. "She lied! She lied to me."

"I hugged her tight. "It wasn't what you thought it would be, was it?"

"It hurt so bad."

"Brooke, you're only thirteen."

"I can't accuse him of anything. The whole school will make fun of me; they'll laugh that I couldn't handle it."

With one arm I pulled her to her feet and guided her toward my car while using a dirty thumb on my other hand to punch Sara's number into my cell phone. "Sara? This is Jules. I'm on my way to the hospital with Brooke. Meet me there."

I was distraught about Brooke. I tried to keep busy at home. I was grateful for chaos at work and for Hudson at the stables. I asked Sara every morning at the gym about her daughter.

"Not good. She breaks down crying without provocation. She doesn't want to go to school. Brad is having her home tutored. He's furious, of course. I guess Kim is suppose to be there when Brooke gets home from school. She said she figured you'd be there so she felt she could do some shopping. He's actually considering an annulment stating child neglect and endangering. Brooke is gloating about that."

"What about her sessions with the psychiatrist?"

"He has her on medication. I'm not sure I like that. There's going to be some shuffling for sure. She might even come back to live with me but she'll have to go back to school if she does. I certainly can't stay home; can't afford a nanny or tutor. So all the uncertainty isn't helping any."

"Could she stay at your parents' place during the day?"

"I really don't think they could deal with her mood swings. I don't think it's fair to ask them at their age."

"Should I go out as usual on Thursday?"

"Check with Brad about that."

Thursday was the first day Mr. Austin actually asked me to stay to help the paralegals just as I was getting ready to leave.

"I'm sorry, Mr. Austin. I have something really important I have to do this evening. If you'd have asked Monday about staying today, we might have negotiated a rate of pay for time helping with their job."

I almost laughed at the way the redness started in his neck and crept up over his face until it reached his scalp just like in the cartoons I used to watch as a kid.

"Negotiate?" he sputtered.

"Well, yes. My salary is for getting my work done. If I'm doing someone else's job, I'd expect overtime at their rate of pay."

"You can stay and help or find another job!"

"Do you want a two week notice?"

The redness deepened a shade as he growled, "Yes."

"Fine. You'll have it in writing on your desk in the morning. Good evening."

I turned on my heel and left the office. I wouldn't swear to it, but though she kept her eyes down, the receptionist's lips seemed to be losing the battle against forming a grin. As I reached forward to push open the plate glass door with Stahlman, Stidd and Austin printed in gold, I noticed my hand was shaking. My arms were so weak I could hardly get the door open. Before I was outside, my knees felt wobbly. By the time I got to my car, I felt nauseous. What had I done? I sat in my vehicle fighting the urge to go back in to offer to help the paralegals another night if he'd just let me keep my job.

Breathe deep, Jules, I encouraged myself. You've been practicing this moment's speech for some time. It was true. I had thought long and hard about what my course of action would be in this event. And if Cindy was right about Hudson sending me messages, strange as it sounded, I had his blessing. Oh, Hudson, I've got to find another job soon or I'll lose you, I moaned. I'd have to start sending out resume's tonight. I had a job for two more weeks. But now, I had that important previous engagement to attend to.

When I pulled into Brad's farm an unfamiliar car was in front of the garage. I saw Kim look out the window. I waved. She scowled and turned away. I couldn't believe that car had never been there all the times I'd gone to ride with Brooke.

Walking to the barn, I saw no horses in the pasture. Had they been sold? I tried not to act surprised when I saw the clean buckets and feed pans. Raven was in cross ties. Brooke stood, brush in hand, forehead leaning against his neck.

"You've got a head start on me," I challenged cheerfully.

"Fred's already groomed.

"Wow. Thanks." I brought Fred out to another set of cross ties to tack him up. Brooke started saddling Raven. I kept glancing surreptitiously at the horses, checking the thoroughness of the grooming. I stretched Fred's legs.

"How do you do that?"

I picked up Raven's knee, worked my hand down to his ankle and gently straightened his leg toward me. "Now you do the other one. Don't yank on it. Slow and gentle." I watched her. "Very good."

Brooke smiled.

It started out as a quiet ride. There was a chill in the air. I was watching the sun settle toward the horizon. The underbellies of the clouds were reflecting pink and gold.

"What are you thinking?"

The voice and the question startled me.

"How much I love sunsets, and riding…and about job hunting."

"You have a job, don't you?"

"I just gave them my two week notice."

"Why?"

"They wanted to take advantage of me."

"Where will you work?"

"I don't know yet. I'll probably start sending out resume's tonight."

After a pause, Brooke asked, "Would you help me learn to post? I never could get on the right diagonal."

I smiled inwardly. "Okay. This is a nice area right here. Walk him out and make a big circle around me. Start whenever you're ready. After you cue him and he goes into the trot, let yourself bounce twice and then post."

She started on the right diagonal but because she was pushing up from her feet, she was soon out of rhythm.

"Whoa, whoa," I called trotting Fred over to her. "Keep your feet soft in the stirrups. Pick yourself up from the knees. Let Raven just stand still while you try that."

She managed a couple good ones and then began to flop back into the saddle. "That's hard," she complained.

"Watch me so you have an idea how it looks."

I trotted a huge circle around her. "Now when you work on it, picture it in your mind. Try again. Remember to bounce twice."

Again, she started good but was soon flopping into the saddle. "I can't do it."

"It takes time, Brooke. Let's just walk and you can practice lifting yourself from the knees a few times. Stop before you feel the need to flop down. That probably doesn't feel good to Raven. Maybe you can do squats to help build up your thigh muscles."

The rest of the ride was quiet with Brooke practicing rising out of the saddle every little while. When we finally dismounted at the barn she groaned, "Ouch. My legs are sore."

I laughed. "They'll toughen up. Just keep at it."

We groomed the horses and fed them. Brooke walked me back to my car. She put her arms around my waist in a hug. "Thanks for coming, Jules."

I hugged her back. "My pleasure. Shall I come next Thursday?"

"Every Thursday."

CHAPTER SEVENTEEN

I was talking a blue streak to Marshall as we drove toward Hoverdale.

"Still no answers on any of the résumé's I've e-mailed. If I don't' have a job when my two weeks are up, I'll have more time to work on my writing."

"How's the novel coming?"

"Good. I'm really liking what I've written. I can't believe I let it go for so long."

"Not scared of being unemployed?"

"Maybe when I actually walk out the door for the last time, the reality will hit me and I'll freak out but right now my writing seems so right. I could almost forget about sending out résumé's."

"How are you going to introduce me?"

My heart skipped a beat. "How do you want me to introduce you?"

Marshall pulled up the console arm between us and retrieved a small black velvet box from the compartment below which he held toward me. "As your Fiancé?" he asked.

I gasped but felt no hesitation in opening the lid. The sparkle as the light reflected from its facets made me smile.

"Is that a yes?"

I transferred my smile to him, leaned over the console and kissed his cheek. "That's a yes."

Strangely the rest of the ride was silent. I kept looking at the ring on my finger, smiling at the sunny landscape we were driving through, smiling at Marshall and rolling the word fiancé' around my mind and over my tongue. It was amazing that the feeling of uncertainty I had when Josh proposed to me was so different from the euphoria I felt now. Marshall kept glancing from the road to me and smiling at my reaction to being engaged to him.

I was relieved as we were driving up the lane to see it wasn't lined with cars like the last time I was here. I hoped the few extra cars parked around the garage belonged to my new-found sisters.

Movement on the big wrap-around porch caught my eye.

"Marshall, do you see that dog on the porch?"

"No. He must have gone over the edge before I looked."

"Yeah, it must have." I smiled as I watched Sophie lying with her paws crossed watching as we continued up the drive. I got the dessert from the back floor of the vehicle. Sidney heard the car doors slam. She came squealing from around the side of the house.

"Here she is. Oh, and the friend. Hello. I'm Sidney."

"Nice to meet you Sidney. I've heard a lot about you."

The smell of grilling steaks filled the air. "Mmmm. Smells like we're just in time," I said.

Mrs. Melesky came to give me a welcoming hug.

"Mom, this is my fiancé, Marshall Provost."

Tears sprang to her eyes as she gave Marshall a hug. "You take good care of our Jewel."

"I plan to."

"Come, come. Meet the rest of the family."

I felt Sophie rub against my leg as we made our way. I surreptitiously reached down to give her a rub behind her ears.

The introductions were over; the meal was delicious; Marshall and Mr. Melesky gravitated to the barn where Dad was restoring a sixty-nine Corvette. Sidney wanted to play bad mitten. I watched as Sophie ran back and forth chasing the birdie as we batted it over the net.

"Where's Bob?" I asked between swings of my racquet.

"Oh, he didn't want to come. Said it was his only day off and he didn't feel like socializing." Sidney's voice strained in an upper octave.

We finished our game and found seats with Dee Dee and Hannah. Mom came out of the house with a bundle. The men came from the barn.

"Jewel, I knitted these hanging hand towels. The knitted part hangs and buttons over cupboard handles. It isn't much, but I'd like you to have them."

"I've seen those. They're so handy. Thank you."

"Jewel, I didn't know you were engaged, but I have a great gift for you. My editor wants to publish your short stories, including the last one, in a collection."

My mouth dropped open. "You're kidding?"

"Nope. He wants to know if you're working on anything else."

"I've started a novel."

"I'll give you Chad Dubiecki's number. Give him a call and tell him what it's about. If you have any completed chapters let him know. He might give you an advance. You could quit your job and work on it full time."

Marshall and I stole a glance at each other and he slipped in a wink.

Sophie was sitting next to my leg with her head laying on my lap; her soulful eyes looking up at me. My mind was jumping with the possibilities of writing full time and my hand was absently stroking the soft curls on her ears.

"Something wrong with your knee, Jules?"

Startled, I looked up at Hannah. She was grinning at me.

"Felt like a love bug ran across it," I grinned back.

The next two weeks were long and hard to get through. My mind felt like a dervish going round and round with my good fortune. I was engaged to Marshall; I was having my short stories published; I was going to meet with Chad Dubiecki about my novel.

Life couldn't get any better. Although I was sometimes distracted at work and everyone knew I had turned in my two week notice, they kept asking why the smile; what was my secret, as though quitting wasn't enough.

There are times when your life comes apart like an atom being split; when those around you disappear as though blown outward by some energy force that had been building up pressure until it could no longer remain contained. Even the weather felt like the aftermath of the explosion with hazy skies and heat waves visible above sidewalks and car hoods.

During my last week at Stahlman, Stidd and Austin, I found out they would be defending Greg in his rape trial. I thought it was a sign that leaving the office was the right course of action for me and quieted the unease of not having a steady paycheck.

Brad had his marriage to Kim annulled. He took a job with a group of attorneys in Damascus in order to give Brooke a new start with some anonymity. His farm appeared on the real estate market.

Brooke had begun to rely on Raven for companionship. Because she was taking good care of both horses, Brad found a boarding stable close to Damascus so Brooke could keep him. I quickly made inquiries. A new addition to the saddle club would be welcomed. Although I was in transition and my finances were unstable, I strongly felt purchasing and donating Fred was the right thing to do. Brad gave me a good price on him just to expedite the release of his responsibility for the horse.

I went to Arielle's first school show. Although she was thrilled to see me, I discovered she had a boyfriend. Jeremy courted me, showed me around, gallantly disappeared when Arielle and I had a chance to chat. I felt so happy for her. Still I felt I was a chink in the cogs.

Josie's grandfather died so she didn't go on the trail ride. Bob encouraged Sidney to attend since Castle Guard was then available.

He even magnanimously offered to help at the bonfire site. He then had a tryst with Angel out among the tethered horses.

Angel then went back to Alex, who, I learned had taken her back repeatedly.

Sidney retreated to lick her wounds from another betrayal. I called her to apologize.

"For what?" she whimpered.

"For bringing Angel into the proximity of Bob. All I did was set you up to be betrayed again."

"Did you know she was like that?"

"No."

"And you had no idea Bob would want to go to the trail ride. So I'm pretty sure you're absolved."

"Sidney, you are so forgiving. Will you still ride with me?"

"You couldn't keep me from it."

I could hear the smile in her voice and that lifted my spirits in spite of the sweat running down my face and arms.

Lord Baruk stood in his stall waiting for another owner. Angel had pretty much abandoned him, leaving just a note on the cork board outside his stall. "Sell him or give him away."

I felt so bad for him. He was a sweet horse; gave his best, and it seemed to me, he took his frequent change of owners in stride. That is until I found Cindy outside his stall one day as I was on my way to help keep him exercised. She was hugging Baruk's head and crying. I patted Baruk's neck as I knelt beside Cindy. "Cindy, what's wrong?"

"Baruk is so sad because he's alone again. He thinks no one wants him because he isn't good enough."

Tears filled my eyes. "I think he's good enough. I wish I could afford to make him mine."

Cindy looked up at me with hope shining in her blue eyes. "Will you take him?"

"Oh, Cindy, I can't afford to pay for another stall and vet bills and farrier fees."

"My parents say they can't afford a horse either."

"I was going to ride him. Why don't we go ask Shelly and your Mom if you can too?"

Her eyes and mouth popped into big 'O's. "Yes, lets."

We were limited to the arena as 'mom' wasn't sure about Baruk. He was, however, a perfect gentleman. Hudson walked close to Lord Baruk and neither horse flattened their ears in irritation. 'Make him yours' insisted my mind. 'I can't afford another stall even if he's free,' I argued with myself. When I saw Cindy looking at me with a grin on her face, I wondered if it was really myself I was debating with.

Initially I was worried if I'd have the self discipline to write. I discovered it was easy to lose myself for hours in my creation. A break for exercise at the gym or to go riding was enough to energize me for another session at the computer. One session, surrounded by the sound of the air conditioner, was just ending at eight o'clock one evening when the phone rang.

"This is Marshall. Did I interrupt a stream of creativity?"

I laughed. "Just finished. I was getting ready to take a walk."

"It's raining and is suppose to storm."

"It's raining?" I looked out the window to see the trees in front of my balcony were dark with wet; fresh from having the dust washed away. "At last," I sighed with relief. "I love walking in the rain. Maybe I'll get back before it storms."

"Have you eaten?"

I paused to recall my last meal. "No. As a matter of fact I haven't."

"Let's go out to eat."

"Sure. I'm going for a short walk..." The doorbell rang.... "I should be back before you get here." I opened the door to see Marshall standing there with his cell phone to his ear.

"I don't think you have time."

"Let me change."

"You're fine. Let's go."

As he escorted me down the steps, he called someone on his cell phone and said, "We're on our way."

"What's up?" I asked suspiciously.

"It's a surprise."

We were headed toward Hoverdale. I wondered if the family and Marshall had cooked up something. It wasn't my birthday so I was clueless.

"How are things going with Cody?"

"Great. I still think you should sponsor one of the girls now that Brooke is gone."

"We'll see."

"What's been happening with you? Did you ride Hud today?"

"Yes but I caught Cindy crying over Lord Baruk. She said he feels like he isn't good enough for anyone to want to keep him."

"Poor fella. What are you going to do about it?"

"I'm thinking I need to get a real job...Excuse me? What makes you think I'm going to do something?"

"I know you. What makes you think you aren't already working a real job?"

"Well, for one thing, it's too enjoyable. The advance money won't last forever and there's no guarantee they'll accept the novel."

"Jules, didn't Chad give you the advance based on the chapters you showed him?"

"Yes."

"I'd say it's a sure thing."

"But it may not sell."

"If Chad wants to publish it, there's a good chance it'll sell."

"So you think I should buy Baruk?"

"I think you should be your own person and do what you need to do."

I felt my heart constrict; my stomach knotted. "My own person? Are we not..." I could hardly verbalize the fear, "...a couple anymore?" I choked.

Marshall snapped his head to look at me, shock written all over his masculine face. His hand grabbed mine. "Jules, yes, we're a couple. An engaged couple. That doesn't mean you can't be yourself."

I audibly exhaled.

"Is that what you thought...that you have to be other than yourself to be my woman?"

"I guess so, yeah. Aren't we suppose to be what the guy wants?"

"You're who I want. If you quit being that, you won't be the woman I fell in love with anymore. I will support you in whatever you feel is important to you."

I was mulling over what he had said as we turned off the road. Ahead was a house with lights shining out a few windows. The porch light welcomed us. Even though it was dark, I recognized the barn. This had been Brad's farm.

Marshall put the gear in park, shut off the motor, turned toward me, and took my hand in both of his. "I realize you might feel some aversion for this place or maybe it won't bother you at all. I know it's a major purchase that we should have discussed but I wanted to surprise you. If you don't like it, we'll rent it out. I already have potential renters, so don't feel pressured."

"It isn't the barn's fault what happened beneath its roof, or the house's fault for what didn't happen within its walls."

Marshall smiled. "Spoken like a true writer."

We went inside to find a table set, a couple of young men dressed as butler's at the ready, and the heavenly aroma of baked bread and roasting meat to remind me just how hungry I was. I had never been inside the house.

"Have we a moment to take a quick tour or are they ready to serve?"

One of the butlers, who heard me ask the question, yelled to the cook. "How long Joyce?"

Marshall mumbled to me, "Good help is hard to find."

I hid a smile behind my hand.

"Twenty minutes," Joyce yelled back.

"Marshall grinned. "We've got time."

CHAPTER EIGHTEEN

The dinette set where we ate beneath a sparkling chandelier while it rained beyond the windows was the only furniture in the house that night. We decided it would be wise for me to move in and spare me the rent on my apartment. Besides, Marshall didn't want the house sitting empty.

It wasn't hard moving my small apartment furnishings into the house. During a break, I stared out the French doors leading to the back patio and the pool beyond. How I wished we were headed into warmer weather so we could open the pool, which had already been winterized. Well, I consoled myself, I would have my riding for during the cold months. Marshall had ordered construction of a one hundred, twenty by one hundred, eighty foot indoor arena to be started.

Over the next few days hay, straw and grain were purchased, and put in the barns and bins. Stalls were cleaned and bedded. Then we were on our way to retrieve the horses.

"I want to run back to the saddle club stables to see how Fred's doing, Okay?"

One of the volunteer instructors had Fred tacked and standing in the arena. A girl about twelve stood facing him, fists clenched, arms folded across her middle, fear and anger alternating on her face.

"Hi Carrie," I greeted the volunteer as I walked to Fred.

"Hi Jules."

"Hello Fred," I said softly. He whickered and I rubbed his forehead.

I looked at the girl. Her brown hair was uncombed and none too clean. Her clothes hung shapelessly on her. "I used to ride Fred before he came here," I said to her. "He's such a good boy. Such a laid back gentleman."

There was no response from the girl.

"He looks big, doesn't he?" I ventured further.

She nodded.

"It feels even scarier when you're on top of him at first," I laughed. "But once you get used to it, it is so fabulous. Want me to ride with you the first time?"

She nodded and slowly took a couple steps straight toward Fred's face.

"Did you know that each horse's eye can see a hundred and eighty degrees? Because they're a prey animal they need to be able to see all around their body. But they have two blind spots. One is directly behind them, which is why you should always let them know when you're going back that way. You can do that by keeping your hand on them as you move around." I demonstrated and came up on his other side. "The other spot is directly in front of them so you should approach them at an angle. Move this way a bit."

She took a step to the side. I went to her and put my arm around her shoulders but didn't try to force her forward. "Let's go meet him, shall we?"

Finally she took hesitant steps and reached one hand out to touch his cheek.

"Now move your hand down his neck. Pinch him along his crest. That's this area right along here where the mane meets the neck. They like that. Ready to mount?"

She had to stretch to grip the saddle horn of the western saddle and could barely reach the stirrup with her foot. She pulled herself up, and swung her leg over Fred's back. As she landed with a thump in the saddle and saw how high she was from the ground, she grabbed the saddle horn with both hands, Terror contorted her face.

"Okay, I'm coming up. You need to remove your foot from the stirrup so I can use it."

I swung up behind the girl, settling myself behind the cantle, took my foot out of the stirrup so she could put hers back in. I took the reins, turned Fred and we started around the arena at a walk. Her body was rigid as she fought the sway of the horse's steps

"Relax. Let your body move with the rhythm of his."

It took awhile but little by little, I saw her try to do as I had asked. Then I saw the girl's ears move as her face split into a grin and her shoulders let go of the fear.

"Now you take the reins."

Her shoulders tightened again as I transferred the reins from my hands to hers but she didn't resist.

"Don't pull back on them. Horses like soft hands. When you come to a corner look in the direction you want him to go. That automatically shifts your weight. Then use your inside heel, that's the one toward the inside of the arena, to gently touch his side back toward his flank. That'll move his hips over. Horses actually turn by their back side, rather than their front."

After once around and she had relaxed again, I said, "Okay, I'm going to get off."

"No, don't," screamed the girl.

"What's your name sweety?"

"Sharla Walters."

It was barely a whisper and I wasn't sure I heard right. "Did you say Sharla?"

She nodded.

"Okay Sharla. You'll be fine. See what a steady fella Fred is? Trust him and trust yourself." I slid off. "Remember, soft hands. I'll walk beside him. Go ahead; give him a squeeze with your legs."

Her face had the frozen look again as we started off but when I looked back the second time, the smile was back. "Okay, this time you ride him around without me. Keep him close to the wall. Don't let him cut the corners."

The smile was even bigger when she returned.

"There you go," I smiled up at her. "You be good to Fred, Okay? He's a friend of mine."

As I started to walk away, she shouted, "Can't you stay?"

"I have to move my horses to their new home but I'll stop in to see how you're doing occasionally."

Carrie spoke up, "Sharla, why don't you take him around again."

As Sharla and Fred moved off, Carrie turned to me. "Jules, I can't seem to connect with Sharla like you just did. Why don't you sponsor this one? I already have two others. Three is just too many but I didn't want them to turn her away."

Marshall was suddenly at my side and put his arm around my shoulders. I looked up at his brown eyes and he winked. "Okay. Let her know I'll be here next Friday."

We were just finishing the dishes; getting ready to settle down to watch the movie Marshall had brought with him.

"So, when do you want to get married?"

"New Year's eve, right after midnight," I replied.

Marshall went solemn.

"Too soon?" I worried at his silence.

"Hon, I can't do that. How about Valentine's Day."

"No. To clichéish."

"June?"

"Too typical. How about the first day of Spring?"

"I like that." He paused. "The reason I can't do New Year's eve is because my best friend, Jake Andrews, had plans to marry Madison Kurt on a New Year's day. His car was hit by a drunk driver as he was on the way to the New Year's eve party they threw for their friends and family. They were going to slip upstairs and come back to the party in gown and tux just after midnight to get married by the preacher they had invited who knew the plan. Everyone at the party headed for the hospital with Madison. Jake died before they arrived."

"Oh Marshall, that's so sad. I'm sorry."

"Yes, it was hard on a lot of people. Jake was a great guy. He didn't have to be macho. He was comfortable with who he was.

He really liked people. You'd have liked him. Jake had waited for Madison while she went through vet school. They worked together to get Phoenix Stables up and running. They had a special relationship. His death just about killed her."

"And she never remarried?"

"No. I've heard there's one special love for a person. The rest are just pretend." He looked at me and saw the question in my eyes. "You're my special one."

Mom and Dad were in Florida visiting friends, so I invited Hannah, Dee Dee and Sidney to the house I now occupied for a glamour party of a famous line of cosmetics. After the demonstrator left, the real fun started. We had rented chick flicks and tearjerkers to watch. We made pizza and popcorn, ate ice cream smothered in hot fudge. We laughed until we cried; groaned about our nighttime indulgence and slept late. The next afternoon, as we separated to our individual lives again, we swore to diet, and Sidney promised to come ride Lord Baruk to help keep him in shape for me. Josie would have to find another co-leaser for Castle Guard.

The skies were grey for days on end. The chill in the air turned noses red. The leaves lost their green but had not yet found their robes of orange, yellow or vermillion.

I was a bit sad to no longer be among the friends at Phoenix. I was not sure of my new path. It pleased me that CastleontheHudson and Lord Baruk seemed content in their new home but I felt I was leaving an important part of my life behind. When I tried to think of who I had left behind, however, I realized it was more the friendly atmosphere that I missed. I had seldom seen Madison, though her essence seemed to coat everything. I only waved to Shelly who was always circulating about the grounds keeping everything running smoothly. She already had new boarders in the stalls Hudson and

Baruk had once occupied. I still saw the ones who sponsored kids in the saddle club and worked with them on the same night that I was there with Sharla

Sharla was losing her frown and, although she still had trepidation about being so high on Fred's back, she was making progress fast. She was good, though a bit lethargic, at grooming and tacking up. Most of the credit went to Fred for building her confidence by being such a steady, calm horse.

One Friday on the way to Phoenix, I picked up several pizzas and put them in the lounge. When the saddle club van pulled in, I waved Sharla toward the lounge. "How about some pizza before we ride?"

"Sure."

There was eagerness in her voice. She ate with gusto and I wondered whether her thinness was because she didn't get enough food. Maybe hunger was why she seemed distracted at times. Indeed, her grooming was more energetic. When we finally showed up in the arena, we made sure we let the rest of the gang know about the pizza. They all quit a bit early to indulge. It was just Sharla, Fred, and me in the arena. We were still working at the walk. Sharla seemed more focused and alert. I also noticed her posture was much better today, and again I wondered if it was because she had the strength, since eating, to hold her body upright?

"Can you lift your body out of the saddle from the knees?" I called to her.

She tried but put her weight in the stirrups.

"Keep your feet light in the stirrups. Squeeze your knees and lift up from there."

She tried again and succeeded.

"Good. Let him take a step and rise again; step and rise."

I let her do it about four times. A moist sheen appeared on her forehead."

"Okay, let's try a trot."

Her facial muscles tightened. "I don't think I'm ready. What if he runs off with me?"

I knew Fred would do no such thing but to allay her fears, I said, "Aim him toward me. I'll stop him. Remember to keep your posture and keep your hands still and down low near the horn. Go ahead and nudge him."

Fred gently went from a walk into a trot. Just before he reached me, I said, "Squeeze the reins."

Sharla squeezed her fingers around the reins and Fred easily stopped in front of me. "That was great Sharla. Shall we end on that positive note?"

I could see her nod was reluctant.

"It'll give you a good image to hold in your mind until next week."

We walked Fred to the grooming bay.

"So how's school?"

"Not too good."

"What are you having trouble with?"

"Everything. I really try to pay attention but my mind just wanders."

"To where?"

"Since, I've met Fred, I think of him a lot. I guess I day dream of being a really good rider on him."

"That's a good goal, but you need to get your grades up too, don't you, to participate in the saddle club?"

"Yeah, and do community service." She looked crestfallen.

"What's the problem?"

"I don't know where to do community service?"

"Didn't they tell you about the list on the bulletin board?"

"Oh. I must not have been paying attention." Her face turned crimson.

"Sometimes when a person is anxious about a new situation it's hard to remember everything you're told. Or if you start to worry right away about something you hear, you don't hear what's said next. Do you live in Montaine, Sharla?"

"Yeah. Decker Street."

"Do you think your parents would allow you to meet me at the library twice a week? Maybe I can help you with the grades."

"They don't care what I do as long as I'm home by eight o'clock."

"Let's see if we can switch your saddle club to Tuesday night and then meet at the library on Wednesday and Friday after school. Now let's go check that list for a community service you can do on the weekend."

Thursday morning, I explained to Sara that on Wednesday and Friday I'd be hitting the gym later in the afternoon so I could use one trip into town for both gym and meeting with Sharla.

"That's great Jules. I'll bet you'll enjoy mentoring that girl."

"How's Brooke doing?"

"Good. Brad said the grades are up and she's really involved at the stables. She's earning extra money grooming other people's horses. She's using the money to pay for lessons and accessories. She might be showing this summer."

"Wonderful. We'll have to go watch."

"That would mean so much to her, Jules. Whenever we talk on the phone or she comes up for a weekend visit, she says she misses you."

"Maybe the next time she comes up, she could come ride with me? Our arena is almost complete."

"She would love that."

"How is Brad doing? Does he like being in a partnership?"

"It isn't much different. Their partner that did Brad's line of work retired. No one else wanted the 'boring stuff', so the clientele is already established. Some of his clients from up here still want his representation. So he's actually doing better. And I think he's taking more time with Brooke."

"How's it going with Justin?"

"I don't see him anymore. He had jealousy and possession issues. It was Brad all over again only worse."

"I'm sorry Sara."

"I'm not. I feel so much better with some time to myself. Heather and I are enjoying some outings. I have time to actually read a book and I'm getting involved in a women's group at church."

"Sounds healthy. We need to go out again."

"Anywhere but Bubba's," she laughed.

Sharla looked lethargic when she shuffled into the library. I had the feeling a tutoring session wouldn't help much if she couldn't concentrate.

"Gosh, I'm famished," I said. "What do you say we start this session over at Grandma's Diner?"

"I don't have any money."

"That's okay. I'll buy. Come on."

After eating, we nursed hot chocolates as I tried to help her get the gist of her math problems, showed her how to take notes in history and social studies, and explained nouns, verbs, adjectives, and adverbs for diagramming sentences in English. After she finished her math homework, I suggested she go to the library where it would be quiet to actually read her history and complete her English assignments. I told her to find me in the library parking lot on Friday. She agreed and I left.

Friday I took a picnic of hot soup, bologna sandwiches, and carrots with veggie dip. After eating we went into the library to begin work. She showed me the notes she had taken in her classes. We went over the mistakes on her math and I tried to explain the next problems. She was having trouble with basic multiplication so I said I'd pick up some flash cards to work on those. I quizzed her on spelling words and suggested she start at the beginning of her history book and take notes until she was caught up.

She groaned. "That's so much work."

I laughed. "But you'll be so glad when you get a good grade on mid terms. Besides, you aren't that far into the book. You'll be caught up in no time."

She heaved a heavy sigh.

"Are you ready for community service tomorrow?"

"No. What if I can't do it?"

"What's hard about walking a Chihuahua?"

Sharla giggled.

"And remember to be nice to Mrs. Spangler. Maybe she'll let you do the dishes too."

Sharla dropped her forehead down to her crossed arms on the table. "Noooo."

"Are you looking forward to the Halloween party at the Saddle Club?"

Her head popped up. "Yes! Can you imagine having to play the games on a horse? It's going to be so fun."

I grinned at her enthusiasm. "I gotta go. See you next Tuesday at saddle club. Come to the lounge first."

My life was flowing smoothly. I was happy. I rode one of my horses in the morning and the other in the evening, alternating so they wouldn't get entrenched in a routine. Sidney came about once a week for a ride. While the weather held we were riding the fields. The arena wasn't quite finished but could be used when the weather was foul.

Marshall and I felt comfortable with just hanging out together. We discussed creating a cross country course on the farm. One weekend, Marshall had brought Cody over to work on assembling model cars. He even gave him a lesson in photography and discovered the child had a good eye for photo composition. I posed for him and was pleased with the proofs.

We were discussing Thanksgiving plans. Of course, I wanted my sisters there but Dee Dee would be on the west coast on a book signing tour. Hannah had a conference to attend the few days before and preferred to use the day to rest before going back to work. And Sidney and Bob always went to his sister's place each year. Marshall had no close relatives to consider. So we were contemplating inviting Fisher, Cody and his single mom, and maybe Sharla.

I had a meeting with Chad to show him the next several chapters on which I had done several rewrites. He informed me that the collection of my short stories was about to go on the market.

Brooke had come for a visit and rode Lord Baruk. She was quite changed. The brat was gone and in her place was a solemn child that took everything seriously. Her riding skills had tremendously improved. Her mind, however, at times seemed far away. I wondered if this would be a part of her life she would block out as I had done or if she still had a good grip on the present.

My efforts at tutoring Sharla were already showing results in higher grades on her homework and tests. I was feeling pretty smug about it. Actually, seeing her efforts made me want to do more for her. I thought I'd have to go meet her parents if I was going to carry out my plans. Marshall thought they were good ideas and that bolstered my resolve.

I almost lost that resolve, however, when I pulled up in front of her home. Why did I think her background would be low income; underprivileged? The allotment contained huge homes with BMWs and sport cars sitting in front of three-car garages with cemented driveways. My knees were weak as I walked to the front entrance and rang the doorbell. A cloud passed over the sun and I felt a shiver thinking it an ominous sign.

A curvaceous woman with long, wavy, blond hair flung open the door releasing wafts of a powerful perfume. I caught a glance of elegant furnishings behind her.

"Mrs. Walters, I'm Jewel Fitzgerald. I'm Sharla's saddle club sponsor."

Despite the cold air, the woman just stared at me without inviting me in.

"I really like Sharla and was hoping to do a few extra things with her if it's alright with you?"

"As long as she's home by eight o'clock."

The door slammed in my face. I stood for a moment to recover from the shock. A wind kicked up. I could feel my old injuries aching from the cold as I ran for the car and its heater. I had wanted to invite Sharla for Thanksgiving but seeing her home; surely they had their own traditions to observe. Besides, Mrs. Walters hadn't given me much of a chance.

It snowed a few inches the second week of November. The saddle club members that came on Tuesday took a little time after their lesson to scoop up a bit of the wet snow for a snowball fight. Then everyone needed to use the restroom. I took that moment of waiting for the others to ask Sharla what else she thought she'd like to do?

"Gee, I don't know. I only get to do this because it's free."

"Are you enjoying it?"

"DUH!"

I laughed. "Okay. Dumb question. But I want you to make a list of other things you think you might like to do and explore. It can be something you already know how to do or something you want to learn to do."

CHAPTER NINETEEN

I was up at my usual time on Thanksgiving morning. I put thermals on under my jeans and my coveralls over top for cold weather barn work, and went out to see my equine buddies. Huge flakes of snow drifted lazily from the dark sky. The ground was already covered. I gave them their feed and hay and then stood by them in their stalls to groom them as they ate. I had been feeling so grateful the past few days. Now, with the aroma of their breakfast wafting about me, it overflowed as tears from my eyes. I leaned my cheek against CastleontheHudson's warm shoulder.

"Hudson, where would I be if not for you? You've helped me come a long way in the past nine months. Angel sold you to me. I'd better call her today."

I spent time with Lord Baruk, thanking him for the enjoyment he'd brought into my life and the companionship he afforded Hudson. I decided not to mention to Angel that I had him.

I could hear the wind starting to howl around the buildings and decided to turn the two geldings into the arena so they could get a bit of exercise protected from the gales. I led them both at the same time; threw them some more grass hay; gave them each a final pat on the neck before I leaned into the wind to fight my way back to the house. The snow swirled and fox hopped looking as if it was trying to return to the clouds from which it had dropped.

I put on some music and called Angel.

"I didn't expect to hear from you," she said.

"I wanted to be sure you knew how thankful I was to you for selling Hudson to me."

"Is this a Thanksgiving ritual?" she sneered. "You took a useless horse off my hands."

"Oh Angel, he's not useless, he's awesome."

"One person's trash is another's treasure, as the saying goes."

My spirit felt like a balloon that had been pin pricked. "Well, thanks anyway. Have a nice Thanksgiving."

What was it with Angel, I wondered angrily? Was she that unhappy that she had to try to make others unhappy as well? I was determined to shed that mantel of gloom she had dropped over my head. It made me feel like I was suffocating.

I called Sharla next. No one answered. I left a message and my phone number in case she wanted to call me back. I thought they must have left early to spend Thanksgiving with relatives.

This was a holiday, I told myself. I should relax, but I was at an exciting part in my novel and wanted to work on it until guests arrived. Surely that would break loose the depressed feeling. Just as I sat at my computer the phone rang. Usually I wouldn't pick up while I was working but it was a holiday and I hadn't actually started yet.

"Hello."

"Jules, this is Arielle."

"Hey girl. Home for the holiday? Did Jeremy come with you?"

"Yes and no. Maybe he'll come for a few days on Christmas break."

"Can you come for a few hours tomorrow? You can ride Lord Baruk, or are you sick of riding?"

"Are you kidding. When have you known me to be reluctant to ride?'

Having plans to ride with Arielle the next day was all it took to buoy my spirits. I turned on my computer, pulled up the document, reread the last couple paragraphs and let the fingers jump to their task.

At last, I paused to work the kinks out of my neck. The light from the window seemed dim. In a panic, I looked at the time. It was two o'clock. I dashed downstairs frantic that the turkey wouldn't get done in time for a six o'clock dinner.

I heard squeals of laughter coming from the family room. There Marshall and Cody were racing cars on a computer game with a young woman watching them. I hurried into the kitchen thinking I could make up for lost time and pretend I hadn't been caught asleep at the wheel. To my surprise the turkey was already in the oven. I didn't see soiled prep equipment so for a moment I wondered if they called for a catered bird. I checked the refrigerator. No naked bird there so they had to have used the one I bought.

I walked back to the family room. "Hey guys." I smiled and waved at the young woman. There was no answer from Marshall. I leaned down to plant a kiss on his cheek and whispered, "Thanks."

"For what?" he asked never taking his eyes from the screen and leaning into the curves. A bit confused, I extended a hand to the young woman. "Hi. I'm Jewel Fitzgerald. You must be Cody's mom."

"Paula Garner. It was so nice of Marshall to invite us for Thanksgiving. I hope you don't mind?"

I felt a pang of anger. Did Marshall not tell her it was a joint decision? "It's our pleasure. We've invited another guest that should be arriving at some point."

"A childhood friend of yours, Marshall told me."

Was that a sneer on her lips? "That's right. His name is Fisher."

"I hope you aren't trying to match make."

"Nope. Wouldn't dream of it," I said, and thought Fisher was too good for her. "Care for a cup of hot chocolate, tea or coffee?"

"Hot chocolate," yelled Cody without taking his eyes from the screen. "With marshmallows."

"Same here," echoed Marshall.

Paula and I smiled and went into the kitchen.

"So who rescued me and put the turkey in the oven?"

"Marshall and Cody. It's the mystery of the cooking elves."

Even though I had asked, if it was supposed to be a mystery, it upset me that she told me. "Why didn't you let me know you were here?"

Paula rolled her eyes as she said, "Marshall didn't want to interrupt your 'creative streak,' as he put it."

"I really appreciate that," I countered.

Fisher arrived about an hour later and joined the other guys playing Black Jack and then we all played a board game. Paula followed me when I headed for the kitchen to put the rest of the meal together.

"Cody sure is having a good time. I really appreciate Marshall taking time with him."

"He's a great guy."

"I hear you're to be married."

I glanced out the window at the deepening snow. "Yes. I can hardly wait. I'm so fortunate to have met him."

"I hope he's for real."

I looked askance at her. "And why wouldn't he be?"

"Well, guys can put on a show until the knot is tied and then the real them comes out."

"You sound like you're speaking from experience, but I think there are usually clues to warn you. I'm pretty sure I've got the real Marshall."

"Would you want to be told if someone knew he was messing around?"

"If they had their facts straight, then I would definitely not want to be the last to know."

A smile seemed to tug at the corners of her lips. I stared at her until she glanced away and abruptly said, "What can I do to help?"

Tuesday, Sharla seemed distracted. She ate in silence and when we got Fred from his stall, she stood leaning into him, her face against his neck. He turned his head around her thin back as though giving her a hug. I could tell she was trying to pay attention but her eyes would glaze over. I had to call her back to the present when she'd miss a direction I'd given.

As she was putting him away, I asked, "Sharla, are you alright?"

Without looking at me she answered, "Yeah, sure."

"Did you have a nice Thanksgiving?"

A sob caught her off guard and then she couldn't regain control.

"Sweety, what's wrong?"

"I can't tell you."

"Why not?"

"They said if I did I won't be able to come to saddle club anymore."

"Who said?"

She sniffed and straightened her shoulders. "Never mind. I'm okay."

"I don't think you are. You've had a hard time paying attention this evening." A cold fear gripped me as memories washed over me. "Did something bad happen?"

She started crying again and could only nod her head 'yes'.

"Won't you tell me? Maybe I can help."

She looked at me dubiously with red-rimmed, watery eyes and red dripping nose. She sniffed.

"Maybe I can't make it go away, but I can give you a shoulder to lean on to get through it. Sometimes that's a big help."

"They said if anyone found out I'd be taken from them and I wouldn't be able to come ride. They promised they wouldn't let it happen again."

"Secrets are hard to carry alone, Sharla." I saw her resolve do battle and then crumble before the need to share her pain.

"My uncle…." Her face began to turn crimson. She looked down. Her shoulders shook with her sobs.

"Did your uncle touch you inappropriately?"

She nodded. It was barely a whisper, "…more."

My breath caught in my throat. Blackness crowded at the edge of my vision. I forced it back. I had to be here for Sharla. I wanted to scream at her parents for not protecting her; for not even giving her a reasonable home life. The words 'as long as she's home by eight' kept echoing in my mind. I wanted to pulverize the uncle; send him to jail; but I had promised her.

"Are you sure you don't want to tell the police?"

She looked up in horror. "No. You can't. He won't do it again. They said I don't have to go there anymore. I'll tell the police you're lying."

"Sharla, I won't tell." I put my arms around her. She buried her face in the front of my coat and clutched me as if she were drowning.

I was crying when Marshall arrived that evening. He took me in his arms.

"Are you all right?"

I could hear the concern in his voice. "I don't think so. I don't know what to do. I know I should tell someone, but she's right. Saddle club is all she has and she'll lose it if I do."

"Something happened to Sharla?"

All I could do was nod as the tears streamed down my face.

"What will you do?"

"Be her friend. Hope that by letting her talk about it, it will keep her from withdrawing into her shame."

"Sounds like a good plan to me. But there's something more, isn't there?"

I nodded. "Why am I surrounded by young girls being hurt by guys? It's bringing a lot of bad feelings back and causing me to have flashbacks."

"I think because you've been there, you're the most capable to help them. You can honestly say, 'I know how you feel'."

I blew my nose and looked up at him. "Do you really think so?"

"Remember Shelly's husband Connor? He moved to Montaine less than two months before Jake was killed. Turned out the previous year his wife and child had been killed by a drunk driver. He really believed he felt compelled to leave his home state to be here to support Madison through the ordeal of losing Jake. I too, have no doubt we're suppose to use our own pain and our strength to help others. My dad was never around. Mom had to work two jobs so I was on the streets a lot. If it hadn't been for a football coach who said it was okay not to be a jock, to find the passion within and pursue it, I wouldn't be where I am today. That's why I'm involved with the kids in the saddle club.

"In the meantime, take care of yourself too. Why not make an appointment with Alyson to deal with the flashbacks. I'll drive you down and won't say a thing coming home unless you want to talk."

I smiled at him and gave him a hug. "Gosh, I love you."

CHAPTER TWENTY

I was excited as I gave Baruk an after-ride grooming and gave both horses their breakfast. After going to the pool for my swim, and then meeting with Sharla for tutoring, I was going to go Christmas shopping. The town's decorations had been up since Thanksgiving. Holiday music played in every store. I could hear grumbling about the constant seasonal sights and sounds but I loved it all. I even planned on eating at Grandma's Diner afterward because I loved the decorations there. Let the humbugs complain. Nothing could dampen my spirits.

I stomped the snow from my boots and shed my coveralls. I was headed for a shower when I noticed the answering machine blinking. I pressed the 'play' button.

"Do you know who Marshall is with?"

That was all the voice said. My heart pounded. The voice wasn't familiar but Paula's face, a smile tugging the corners of her mouth, flashed into my mind. Stop it, I told myself. I remembered the last time I thought Marshall was with a new girlfriend. It had been a client. I know the real Marshall. I will not doubt him, I stated firmly out loud.

I showered, spent time at my novel, made out my Christmas list, tried to keep the Christmas happiness singing in my heart, but the phone message kept making it miss notes and sound flat.

I put on my coat, grabbed the packed lunch I had for Sharla, picked up my purse and swim bag. I had the door knob in my hand when the phone rang. I decided to let the machine get it but stood to listen.

"Check out Marshall's new plaything at Blossom's toy store."

My heart was racing. Blossom's was in the general area I'd be heading to. I felt the urge to drive straight there. The drive into town was torture. I couldn't help but go out of my way to pass Blossom's on the way to the fitness center. Although I resisted pulling in, I scanned the parking lot. My stomach started burning when I spotted his truck…or one that looked like his.

My swim was distracted. I couldn't get my mind off the phone messages and seeing Marshall's pickup at the store. I fought the inclination to believe he was cheating on me. I knew some men claimed to have sincere love for their wives but felt there was no wrong in dabbling on the side. I just couldn't believe that was Marshall. I remembered his statement that I could be myself and he'd support that. Would he say I had to accept and support his need for extra affairs?

I wished Sara was in the lane next to me, both of us pulling our way through the water like we seemed to have to pull our way through life. I would relax knowing we'd have a good heart to heart after our swim. I knew I could lean on her. Or…would she simply view him as any person capable of duplicity, while my love for him enabled me to see him as an exceptional man and incapable of being so shallow? On the other hand, I was afraid of being humiliated and was decidedly glad Sara wasn't there to see my distress.

The turmoil in my mind and heart was sapping my strength. My strokes through the water were slow and feeble. Enough of this! I actually said it under water sending bubbles to the surface. My mind fought back.

Fact: I saw a truck that looked like Marshall's at Blossom's. Maybe it wasn't his or maybe he's picking up a gift for Cody.

Fact: Two phone messages have hinted that he's cheating on me, but maybe someone is just trying to cause trouble.

Fact: I will believe in him until he gives me definite reason not to.

Now, stroke, pull, kick, kick, kick, stroke, pull.

I didn't quite end my day on the high I had started on but still I was pleased. I had resisted stalking Marshall. I had shopped for his gifts with enthusiasm as if we'd be together the rest of our lives, but acknowledged it might be wise to keep the receipts...in case they didn't fit, of course.

As I sat at Grandma's enjoying chili, salad and the visual effects of the decorations, I thought about Sharla's state of mind. She had arrived at our tutoring session unkempt. I warned her that poor hygiene was a sign of being molested. Someone would notice and social services would get involved. I assured her that she had nothing to be ashamed of. She should hold her head high, be proud of who she was; could be; what she had accomplished. Her grades were up; Mrs. Spangler treated her as a granddaughter, letting her do the dishes and read to her as well as walk the Chihuahua, Mighty Tyke. The elderly woman had already bought her a school logo hoody and a Nancy Drew book besides feeding her nutritious lunches.

"But he made me feel so dirty," she had whimpered.

"No one can make you feel anything. Feeling that way because of his sins gives him power over you. Take back your power by replacing that feeling of being dirty with one of pride by treating yourself with respect."

"I'll try," she had promised.

I took a spoonful of chili, looked at the list of things she wanted to do that I had asked her for: Play the flute, learn to swim, learn to roller blade, get ears pierced, get a pet, learn to jump fences on Fred, go to the movies

The bell jangled over the door and absently I glanced up. Marshall came in and sat on a counter stool. I waited to see if anyone followed. He ordered and started sipping his coffee before I walked over to him.

"Care to join me, good lookin'?"

"Hey you," he said with a smile. "I thought you were going out to eat tonight?"

"I am out. Here. I love the decorations and the music here."

Marshall glanced around and listened for a moment. "Okay; if you say so. You sure you want me to join you?"

"Absolutely."

Marshall motioned to the counter waitress to indicate his move and left her a dollar tip. "So did you get all your shopping done?"

"I did. I had a good time."

"Without me?" Marshall made a pouty face.

"Yep. What about you?"

"I would have preferred being with you."

I felt the jab in my heart as I analyzed that it sounded like an evasive answer. "That's good to know but I think if I'm permitted to have a good time without you, you should be able to have a good time without me."

"I agree but I wasn't having a good time."

"Working late?" I fought to keep my breathing regular.

"Well, it turned out to be quite a chore. Paula asked if I'd help her shop for Cody. I should have taken that as a clue. I mean, a mother should know what would please her kid, right?"

"You'd think so."

"Every time I suggested something, she'd whine about not having enough money as though she wanted me to buy it. And she kept hanging on my arm and saying what a good time she was having. Then she had the temerity to actually say if we went out to eat that would make the evening a swell date. What a shock. I had to get firm and tell her I was a one-woman man and my woman was waiting for me at home."

I realized I had been holding my breath as he described his evening and it uncontrollably expelled in a rush of air.

Marshall looked at me curiously. "Are you all right?"

I nodded and tried to return to a normal breathing pattern before saying, "That was pretty bold of her." It was the nicest thing I could think of to say.

"Or desperate," he rejoined. "It's hard for single mom's to make it on their own. I really feel bad for her and for Cody. What would you say to making them our Christmas project?"

"You mean invite them for Christmas dinner?" I felt short of breath again.

"No. I'm afraid that would make Paula think I was interested in her. Let's get them a few things each. I'll tell Paula we got a few things for Cody and to leave the door unlocked Christmas eve so we can play Santa."

I saw the excitement in his eyes as he planned his excursion. "Their apartment is really drab. I've seen it when I took Cody home a time or two. Maybe you can pick out some furnishings to brighten the place. I'll pay for it all since Cody is my responsibility."

Tears welled up in my eyes.

"What's wrong?" Marshall asked with concern in his eyes.

"I've just never met such a compassionate man. I would love to play Mrs. Claus."

Marshall was silent, not quite knowing what to say.

"It's still early. Want to come out to the house?"

He grinned, relieved at the change of subject. "Sure. I can help carry in your packages."

"No need. I'll get them tomorrow," I assured him innocently.

We shed our coats inside the door of the house.

"I'll make us something hot to drink. What do you want?"

"I'm feeling Christmassy. Hot chocolate with marshmallows. Do you have any Christmas DVDs?"

"Sure. Take your pick."

I was getting the milk from the refrigerator when I heard the answering machine playing back. I realized I had forgotten to clear the messages. I poured the milk into the pan. I put the pan on the burner. I turned the burner to medium. It felt like I was in slow motion.

And then Marshall's arms were around me. He whispered in my ear, "What you must have been thinking all day."

"I was thinking I had a one-woman man who knew his woman was waiting for him."

CHAPTER TWENTY-ONE

"So, what's on your Christmas list?" I asked Sharla.

"Clothes, pierced earrings, roller blades."

"Do you usually get what you ask for?"

"Sometimes. Other times it's like they don't even look at the list."

"What are you getting your parents?"

"Nothing. I don't have any money. I don't get an allowance."

"Would you like to do some barn work to earn some? Then I can take you Christmas shopping."

Sharla smiled. "I think that would be fun."

"Be sure to ask your parents. I can pick you up Saturday morning."

"They won't care."

"Maybe not, but I want them to know where you are, Okay?"

"Sure."

"And let Mrs. Spangler know you'll be there a little later than usual."

I worked her pretty hard. I let her muck both stalls, scrub feed pans and water buckets, wash the mirror in the arena, dust and sweep the judges box and lounge, polish tack and then ride Lord Baruk to exercise him. Of course, I rode Hudson with them.

Baruk was very sensitive to Sharla's cues and she had to force herself to be light with them as Baruk wasn't as forgiving as Fred.

Her initial nervousness about being on a strange horse turned to fear as he quickly responded to cues she didn't know she was giving. It was all I could do to get her to sit still and quit yanking on his mouth in her effort to get him to stop. Finally both were still.

"Pull your elbows back, Sharla. Drop your hands so there's a straight line from your elbow to his mouth. You want to keep that line straight. English is a bit different from western. Now just squeeze your calves until he starts to walk. Let your pelvis sway with his motion but keep your hands near the pommel and that straight line from elbow to his mouth"

"How do I stop him if I'm not allowed to pull on the reins?"

"Stop letting your pelvis move with him. That's called stilling your seat."

Sharla tried it and was amazed. "Oh wow. How come it's different from how I stop Fred?"

"Well, it depends on the discipline in which you're riding and how well the horse is trained. The better trained the better rider you must be. If you want him to turn sharply to the left, lightly touch your left heel back toward his flank and tighten your left hand. That's asking him to give his head to move his hips to the right which aims his body in the new direction. If you just want to go around a curve, then you'll look at where you want to go and lightly squeeze that rein. Remember that looking in the direction you want to go automatically shifts your weight onto that hip. Just like in western, you want him to bend at the poll, not with his neck.

"Well, we've got just enough time to get them groomed before you need to be at Mrs. Spangler's. Do you want to come tomorrow after lunch to work some more?"

"Sure."

"Bring some clean clothes. You can shower here and we'll go shopping before I take you home."

She didn't answer, but the smile on her face said she was in favor of the plan.

"Do you have any idea what gifts you want to get your parents?"

"No."

"What do they enjoy?"

"Dad golf's a lot."

"You could get him some golf balls or a freezable water bottle. What about your mom?"

"Sharla hesitated. "She drinks a lot."

I wanted to put my arms around her. Instead I said, "Don't you dare get her a shot glass."

Sharla put her hand over her mouth and giggled.

"I wish it would snow," said Sharla as we got out of the car.

"That would really make it feel like Christmas, wouldn't it?" I conceded. "Look at that sky. The weather forecast said it was suppose to."

"But they've been saying that all week."

"You're right, they have. But let's not let lack of snow stop us from having a good time."

We wandered the sports and auto aisles getting ideas, followed by jewelry and perfume. Then we tried on clothes and giggled over lingerie. We bought and ate hot pretzels; added turtles and yogurt covered raisins to our bags. She wanted to go off alone for a bit. I used the chance to buy a hoody she had tried on and pierced earrings she had admired. We rendezvoused at the service desk.

"I've decided on the golf balls for Dad," admitted Sharla, "and a necklace for Mom."

"Okay. Let's go get them."

When we came out of the store there was two inches of snow on the ground and the huge fluffy flakes were still falling. Sharla squealed with delight, clapped her hands and jumped up and down.

"Merry Christmas, Merry Christmas."

"Oh the snow makes it so perfect," I sighed in agreement.

We put our packages in the trunk of the car and walked beneath the falling snow, and amid the street and store decorations to Grandma's Diner. We ordered burgers and egg nog milkshakes. The music mesmerized me and I sat musing on the eight foot tree

Marshall and I had shopped for and decorated with the ornaments and lights we had purchased a couple evenings ago. Sharla hadn't seen it yet. I hoped it made her feel as good as it thrilled me.

"What are you thinking?"

Her question startled me. "About the Christmas tree at home that Marshall and I worked on together, and the cookies you and I are going to bake after we're done here. What about you?"

Her face grew solemn. "I wish I could just think of good things."

"Do you have flash backs?"

"Sometimes. But it's more like I'm afraid he's going to show up unexpectedly."

My mind was in turmoil. I didn't know how to help this child. Should I confess my own childhood trauma? I couldn't tell her to just not think about what had happened.

"You know Sharla, I was raped when I was twelve also." The tears started streaming down my face. "So I really do understand what you're going through."

When I finally composed myself enough to look at her, her face was ashen.

"Weren't you always afraid?"

"I don't remember. The foster family that took me in said I was very withdrawn. I was very good at focusing on other things. I got straight A's in school, was on the swim team, got all kinds of ribbons in horse shows. So I guess you could say I just blocked it all out by totally concentrating on whatever I was working on at the time. I'm not sure that was a good way to handle it because I eventually forgot my foster family and a dear friend when I went on to college because then I was so focused on my classes there. I even forgot I could ride a horse. But at least I don't remember being scared all the time."

"I really try to concentrate on school work, but if you weren't helping me, I don't know how I'd be doing."

"What would happen if he did show up in your life?"

"I'd be so afraid of him grabbing me."

"A sly grin crept across my face. "What if we took a self defense class? I've always wanted to do that."

153

Sharla's eyes sparkled. "That would be great."
"You know you have to get your parents' permission."
"They don't care…"
We finished in unison…. "As long as I'm home by eight."

It was a morning gym session. Sara was jogging on the treadmill next to me. "Brooke's coming home this weekend."
"How's she doing?"
"Wonderful. The doctor has her in group therapy now."
My eyes lit up. "Wow. What else does he have her doing?"
"Writing in a journal and being a support for the other kids outside of group."
"What do you mean being a support for the others?"
"Listen, sympathize, encourage. Of course, they do that for her also. She says she really likes being able to help others. She says she knows it's a bit early to choose a career but she's thinking of being a psychologist."
"Sara, I know a young girl that has recently been raped by a relative. Her parents have threatened to take saddle club away from her if she tells, but they promised to keep him away from her. I know I should report it but I think it would do more harm than good, as long as they keep their promise to keep the uncle away. Do you think she and Brooke could get together? Maybe Brooke could give her some pointers on how to deal with it."
"Well, they have to be okay with talking about it first. Have her start a journal and be her confidant. The feelings of fear and anger have to be validated before they should try to be strong."
"Gee, that's exactly what Alyson did for me. I should have known that."
"Jules, you were just making headway with your own issues when Brooke needed you. And now you have another needing you. You are such a strong woman."
I didn't feel strong…yet. That vision of me popped into my head occasionally but mostly I felt like a blind person in a dark room. I

worried about Sharla not getting help. I watched her struggle with basics like hygiene and schoolwork when she was feeling vulnerable. Fred, however, seemed to be able to hold her attention and I could see remarkable improvement in her riding skills.

Her parents had signed and even paid for the self-defense class even though it would last until eight thirty in the evening. We were both excited about starting in January. I got her a blank book for her journal writing. She opened it immediately and wrote: Here I am. SEE ME. Hear me ROAR.

I smiled and said, "I think I'd better get one for myself and write some empowering thoughts like that."

Arielle dropped in for a visit. I asked about Jeremy. She claimed they were more like friends these days. I told her of my upcoming marriage in March and she was happy for me.

Marshall visited until late Christmas eve. We opened our gifts. There was even one from Sharla; a framed picture of her.

"This looks like your work."

"Actually it's Cody's but I'll admit to helping a bit. Which reminds me, I still have my Santa's run to make. See you in the morning."

The next morning, I stumbled out of bed at my regular time to sleepily feed and water the horses. I then climbed back under the warm covers. When I finally awoke, the sun was glinting off a new layer of sparkling snow and I had the urge to go riding. I saddled Hudson and headed out into the winter wonderland. His hoofs kicked up the powdery snow. The reflected sun hurt my eyes. I wondered if Hudson felt the glare as I did.

I had hit a block in my novel. I wasn't sure in which direction to take it. So I had shown Chad what I had up to that point and then checked out some books from the library to give my brain some down time. Now astride Hudson, my mind wandered from Marshall, to Sharla, to Hannah, Dee Dee, and Sidney. The sisters and Bob were coming this evening for Christmas dinner. Mom and Dad were wintering in Arizona.

Hudson and I were almost back to the barn when the next scene of my novel formed in my mind. It would add a whole new element to the story and open many possibilities. I dismounted to slide open the door to the arena. It took awhile for our eyes to adjust to the interior despite the many channels of natural light. As I stood waiting, Hudson kept bumping me with his head.

"What's up, big guy?" And then I knew. "You want credit for giving me the new direction for that novel, don't you? Did you really come up with it? Well, thank you."

We had a good work out over jumps and did some dressage. I cooled him out and turned both horses into the pasture as I could feel the outside temperature rising. The icicles were dripping from the eaves of the stables and arena, and the snow cover was melting to form a wet slush.

Marshall's car was parked by the garage when I headed to the house. I picked up the pace and burst through the door. Marshall whirled away from my explosive entry, knelt and grabbed the lid of a box, quickly put it on as he turned to face me. "Merry Christmas."

"Marshall, we opened presents last night."

"I had one last one."

He held out the box toward me. As I reached for it the lid popped off and there was a curly head; black face with pink tongue; warm, brown eyes, all set off with a pink collar.

"Sophie," I squealed in delight.

"Sophie? You were expecting her?"

"No. The Melesky's had a black standard poodle named Sophie. This one is going to be named Sophie also."

"What if it's a boy?" Marshall chuckled

I paused. "Is it?"

"No."

"Sophie, Sophie, Sophie." The little black body wiggled in my arms and licked my face. Do you have to go potty?"

"She just did."

"Let's see if she can again because of the excitement."

She found the yellow spot she had previously made and squatted again nearby.

"Good girl."

I carried her back inside and found a towel to dry off her wet feet and underbelly. I started picking up slippers, books, newspapers, and pillows from the floor before I let her down.

"Don't clean house today," complained Marshall.

"I'm not. I'm puppy proofing. I hope you got her some toys. I need a shower. Be sure to watch her until I get done."

As I came back down the stairs the phone rang.

"Hello?"

Marshall watched my face go white. "What is it?"

"One moment please." I covered the receiver with a hand. "The molesting uncle has shown up at Sharla's. Her mom wants to know if she can come here until he leaves."

"You bet."

I smiled at him and put my hand on his cheek. "We'll be right there. It'll take us a half hour. Will she be alright?" I paused listening. "Okay." Turning to Marshall as I hung up the receiver, I said, "We need to take your truck. Sharla's going to start riding her Christmas bike this way."

"Good thing the roads are clear."

"Come on Sophie."

Sharla had made good time on her bike. As she zipped past us, Marshall made a U-turn on the deserted road and caught up with her. At first I was concerned about the expression on her face but as Marshall hoisted her bike into the truck bed, Sharla climbed into the cab, and Sophie's tongue encouraged giggles from her.

"Merry Christmas Sharla."

Her face went solemn as she ruffed Sophie behind her ears. "It would have been if HE hadn't shown up. I was the one who answered the door. I was so scared when I first saw him. He said, 'how about a kiss for your uncle?' I just slammed the door in his face and walked away. He opened the door and walked in yelling that I needed to learn some manners. I was standing next to mom and whispered, 'You promised.' She got out our personal phone directory. I was surprised she had your number, but I wasn't going to stick around to ask why."

I remembered the time I called their place on Thanksgiving and left my number on their answering machine. "Well, it's great to have you visit. You can help wear out this puppy."

"What's her name?"

Sharla seemed a bit nervous around Bob. I didn't blame her. She stayed near me and there were times I literally put myself between them to make her feel more secure. She kept her eye on Sophie and took her out each time she saw her sniffing around, right after a play session or when the puppy woke up from a nap. When the guests left, Sharla came into the kitchen where I was washing the dishes. She picked up a towel and started to dry what was in the drain rack.

"Jules, thanks for letting me come. I really had a good time."

"Our pleasure. It's getting late. Shall we call your parents and see if you can spend the night? We'll take you home before noon if the coast is clear."

Her face brightened. "That would be wonderful."

"By the way, thanks for the picture. It's a really good one of you."

"Marshall said it show's horse power. What does he mean by that?"

"A woman who knows what she wants, knows she's worth it and goes and gets it."

She smiled. "Really?'

"Yep. Like tonight. You demanded boundaries because you knew you deserved them. That show's you're healing."

"But I don't know what I want to be."

"You don't have to immediately know your whole life. Just one step at a time."

"Like tonight?"

"And like the defense class and being brave enough to learn how to ride a horse. Remember how afraid you were of Fred?"

"Yeah. Horses are so big."

"Are you still afraid?"

"Only of horses I don't know."

"The more horses you ride the better rider you'll be. You won't believe it, but when I first got Hudson, I was afraid of him too."

"No way!"

"Yep. So what did you get for Christmas?"

"The bicycle. I love it. In-line skates and a coupon to get my ears pierced."

"Wow. You really made out."

"I know. I love the earrings you got me. I can't wait to wear them. Did you notice I'm wearing the hoody you got me?"

"I did."

"Jules, could you teach me how to cook?"

"I'm not sure how good a cook I am. Maybe we could each find recipes and make them together."

"That would be fun."

"Why the sudden interest in cooking?"

"It isn't fair that you and Mrs. Spangler feed me all the time."

"But you look so much better and aren't so lethargic."

"I know. I had no idea that was why I was so tired. But I thought if I could learn to cook, I won't have to mooch off you and maybe I could get my parents to sit down to a meal together occasionally."

I wrapped my arm around her neck to pull her close. The suds on my hand slid to her chin leaving a bubbly beard. "Horse power," I whispered in her ear.

CHAPTER TWENTY-TWO

New Year's eve the temperatures dropped to zero and stayed there, and below, for weeks. I rode my horses only in the arena, and they were turned out in winter blankets. Sidney came on Saturdays to ride with me. Sophie was growing; was house broke; was well mannered. Sharla and Brooke finally got together and remembered each other from school. Although not friends before because of being a year apart, their common trauma drew them together.

The third week of January, Sharla showed me her end of term grades and announced she was ready to try it on her own.

"Good for you! I'm sure you'll do fine."

"I'm sure also."

"That sounds like horse power," I smiled.

"I know. Brooke calls it positive thinking. She says I should picture in my mind what I want to be and then act as if it were true."

"That sounds like good advice. You're doing it already aren't you? You are blooming like a summer flower with its face to the sun."

She smiled in pleasure and gave me a hug. "I couldn't have done it without you. Thank you so much Jules."

"Well, instead of a tutoring session, let's go celebrate at Grandma's Diner."

Sharla seemed to shift gears then. She took care with her appearance and accepted responsibility for getting enough to eat.

She was really focused on caring for and learning to ride Fred, and enthusiastically threw herself into her self-defense class. We planned to get together once a month to cook a whole meal together. Marshall and Cody were invited to eat. Every weekend, however, after walking Mighty Tyke in his boots and fleece coat, she got a baking lesson from Mrs. Spangler.

I found a calf length dress to use as my wedding dress. It had slim bright yellow ribbons around the waist that tied and hung to the side in front. The sleeves were long but sheer. I pleased Sidney by asking her to be my matron of honor and if she'd take care of the horses and Sophie while we were on our honeymoon. Marshall had a friend lined up to be our photographer. Connor was to be his best man. Sara's preacher agreed to marry us in their church. Sara and Heather offered to decorate the hall and prepare the food.

My collection of short stories was on the market and actually selling. Despite the frigid temperatures, my life and writing flowed like a spring stream.

I was pulling in at Phoenix stables behind the saddle club van one Tuesday afternoon. The Phoenix four-horse trailer was parked and unloading new horses. Stable hands stood nearby holding Fred, Roxy and Spiffy Zip. As I got out of my car, I heard Sharla frantically calling Fred's name as she ran to him. Fred raised his head at her voice.

"Where are you taking him?" she almost screamed.

Madison put her hand on Sharla's shoulder. "Honey, we called your house yesterday to say Fred was going for a rest and that he wouldn't be here for you to ride. Didn't they pass on the message?"

"He'll be back?"

"Yes, he will. Cindy tells us when the horses are tired. They work really hard for us. These three will go someplace to rest for about a month."

I could see the tears welling in Sharla's eyes. "I can't ride for a month?"

"I'm really sorry but we have to be considerate of the horses."

"I understand."

Madison looked at me. "Sharla was supposed to call you about not riding. I'm sorry you made the trip for nothing."

"I don't mind. We'll just hang out for a bit. Looks like you got some new horses."

"Yes. Unfortunately, none of them are suitable for saddle club. We are looking, however. Poor Roxy and Spiffy Zip are getting up in years. They can only take beginning students once a day."

"When they're ready to retire, let me know. I'll take them as pasture companions."

"Thanks Jules. That's a relief off my mind."

Madison turned her attention back to the new horses and I turned to Sharla. "Shall we wander around? Let's go see who's in the stall Hudson used to have."

She brightened a bit. "Okay."

A big grey named Attica stood munching hay in the stall. Sharla reached out to pet the well-muscled neck. "Do you think I'll ever be able to ride a big horse like that?"

"He isn't much bigger than Fred. How badly do you want it?"

She smiled and said, "Bad enough to picture it in my mind."

"You know, Sharla, maybe it's time you moved on from Fred. Remember when you said you'd like to learn to ride English rather than western?"

"Yes."

"Maybe now is the time to switch. Maybe you've outgrown saddle club."

"I thought I could stay in it until I graduated."

"I don't mean physical age. I mean mentally. I know your home life still isn't wonderful but you're taking responsibility for your own well being. That shows maturity. Maybe your parents would let you do barn work in exchange for lessons. You could come in the saddle club van but they'd have to pick you up. What do you think?"

"I could ask."

"If they say no, you can always continue in saddle club after Fred comes back. Let's go check the bulletin board to see what day they have an opening."

I was driving home before I realized I had offered a home for the two aging horses without worrying about what Marshall would think. Horse power, I whispered to myself with a smile. I'd tell him of course, and alter the plans if he preferred I not take the horses, but somehow I knew he'd support my endeavor. I could always use them for small visitors occasionally.

February continued bitter cold but warmed toward the last week. I was putting in long hours on the novel before Marshall showed up in the evenings for dinner. I was getting a good taste of what married life was going to be like and I loved it. Marshall and I were so comfortable with each other, we didn't have to be talking or doing something all the time. But when we did talk it was interesting and revealing conversation. He wanted a room in the basement to set up as a dark room as well as an office for his real estate business. I was so happy that our dreams were pulling us into closer proximity rather than pushing us away from each other.

We were both enjoying Sophie who was growing fast, and I was enjoying not being so busy. Sidney still came to ride, but Sharla was enjoying the work/ride program at Phoenix, and so far her mother hadn't forgotten to pick her up from there. Her work sessions and lesson were on Friday evenings. Marshall's saddle club session with Cody was on that evening as well. So one evening I came along to sneak a peak at Sharla's lesson.

I caught a glance of her scrubbing buckets in the heated stock room before I slipped in to hide in the judges' box. I knew it would be awhile so I pulled out a paper back novel to read. A chapter later Shelly came into the enclosure high above the arena and sat next to me.

"Marshall said you came along to see how Sharla was doing."

"How is she doing?"

"So far, pretty good. She's still insecure with new things but it doesn't take her long to settle in. I don't think she'll go back to saddle club." She paused. "That'll free up Fred for another child. And we found two more horses to add to the saddle club stables."

I held my breath as she continued.

"So we have room for at least three more kids that will need sponsors. The kids are already chosen. They're here learning to groom but we need more sponsors."

My mind was spinning with the remembrance of how much time I had spent with Sharla and how much I was enjoying that time to myself now. As Sharla led Deek into the arena, Shelly chuckled as she got up to leave. "I'll leave so you can stew and feel guilty."

Deek was well groomed and I was proud of the job Sharla had done. Using the mounting block, she was soon astride. The line was straight from her elbow to Deek's mouth. Her body was held with confidence, her legs lying still along his barrel. Deek stood waiting. With the squeeze of Sharla's calves, Deek moved into a walk. As she went around the far end of the arena and started back, she was looking for the dressage letters along the top of the arena wall and caught sight of me. I raised my fist, palm out, toward her and mouthed 'horse power'.

She smiled and nodded. That's when I remembered the satisfaction I'd gotten from spending time with her. My mind countered that the next one may not be as rewarding. I could always say no but it wouldn't hurt to go look over the new kids on the block. Sharla's concentration was back on her riding. Now would be a good time to slip out.

I entered the saddle club stable area. Along the aisle three horses of varying sizes stood in cross ties being groomed by three girls. As I walked down the aisle, ducking beneath cross ties, I saw eyes watching me; sullen, curious, disinterested. Would three sponsors come forward? I had heard Diane say she sponsored two, and remembered when Carrie was juggling three until I took Sharla.

Rising above the swish of brushes, and my own thoughts was a voice that rang with enthusiasm and cheerfulness. It reminded me of a bubble and when I got to the horse last in line, I almost had to laugh. She looked about ten and was even shaped like a bubble; roley poley; blond, bouncy curls. Her eyes were round with excitement, her cheeks plump and pink, her mouth open, open, open as she flitted around her small horse touching the brush here, giving a stroke there, squatting to do a leg and then up to fluff the mane. The horse's eyes were showing the whites, its feet stomped and the body kept trying to move away from the spastic child as though trying to get away from a swarm of blood sucking horse flies.

"We are going to be best friends aren't we Polly? I just moved her with my mommy and daddy."

I looked the other girls over carefully and then went to Shelly's office. "I'll try taking the serious ones if they're both on the same nights. Is that possible?"

"You bet. Are you sure?"

"No, but I don't want any of them turned away."

"Can you take the three temporarily?"

"Whew, that would be rough. Are you sure it would be temporary?"

"Well, I can't promise but I'll do my best."

"I'm not sure I can focus the bubble."

Shelly laughed, but I could feel my shoulders tighten from the thought of the challenge that was being set before me. "Jules, you put in an awful lot of time with Sharla. We only ask that you be here on Wednesday evening for these girls. The rest: grades and community service is up to them. Pace yourself."

Shelly, of course, had no idea of the extent of my concern and involvement with Sharla. I gave a wry grin. "I'll do my best."

Marshall was just getting in his truck when I left Shelly's office. I climbed in beside him. He gave me a hug and a kiss. "How'd it go?" he asked.

"I'll get three started, just until more sponsors are recruited."

He whistled. "Whew, you're more woman than I am."

My worry prevented a smile. "Well, Shelly said not to take on so much responsibility for them. I should let them worry about grades and community service."

"Think you can do that?"

"I'm sure I'll help if they need it. We'll be here on Wednesday evenings. I didn't realize the horses had more than one rider."

"It started out one on one but the horses were idle all week. The kids came only on weekends. We can get more kids involved if we do three to a horse. A different child on each horse on Monday, Wednesday and Friday. There are Play Days on the weekend during the summer, if you remember. The horses get every other day off so aren't really over worked."

"We'll be getting married in a few weeks. We'll miss those two weeks we'll be gone."

"It won't hurt the kids."

"I can hardly wait."

"To start these three girls or to marry me?"

I punched his arm. "What do you think?"

"Seriously, hon, we need to talk about the children issue. I told you I didn't want any at this late date. Are you okay with that?"

"There are plenty of kids in our lives, and I certainly don't fantasize about having any. When we had that initial conversation, I didn't feel disappointed, so I think you're safe."

CHAPTER TWENTY-THREE

A curtain of grey dropped in front of the sun one day and forgot to lift again. The snow fell…and fell. The wind howled. The temperature plummeted. We stayed in if at all possible and when we had to go out, we hunched into our coats, shoulders stiff against the frigid cold. We even folded our arms across our bodies as though not trusting buttons, zippers or Velcro to keep the winter wear in place.

I couldn't help thinking of my fast approaching wedding. My vision of the day was of the sun coming out to bless our union, and its warmth bestowing a happily-ever-after benediction. I just couldn't believe there would ever be another cold day after March nineteenth.

I thought over the past year and felt healed and whole. It seemed I had shed my insecurities and had assumed adulthood. My marriage would be a culmination of my journey. I will have arrived. The vision kept me moving through the dim overcast days.

Mom and Dad returned from their travels. We had dinner with them one evening. Everyone enjoyed Sophie. When arriving, I had seen the original Sophie, my ghost companion, watching from the porch. But when she saw little Sophie bound from the car, she turned and trotted away. I felt a stab in my heart thinking I had offended her.

After dinner Hannah quietly asked if I could see big Sophie.

"She was on the porch when we pulled in, but when she saw little Sophie, she left. Have I driven her away?" I felt tears filling my eyes.

"Maybe she just feels she can go to her rest now that you have little Sophie."

"Oh, I hope that's it."

We gradually absorbed Marshall's things into the house we would soon be jointly occupying. There wasn't much left at his apartment besides a bed and dresser, but suddenly he wasn't coming to share evenings with me. At first it was just random occasions but then it progressed to several evenings in a row. The times he did arrive, he was taciturn. I was afraid he was getting cold feet. Maybe he was having a last fling. Paula's face flashed into my mind.

My first response was to call his place. His answering machine picked up. "Marshall, this is Jewel. I just thought I'd make sure you're all right. Have a good night. I love you." He never returned the call. I had let him know I was concerned. That's all I could do.

A few nights later, however, I had a strong urge to drive past Paula's place. So much for conquering your insecurities, I admonished myself. Then I started chanting to keep myself sane. 'Whatever you love, you must set free. Whatever you love, you must set free.' I'd make a cup of tea and pick a book to read. Or I wrote frantically, often throwing whole pages away and starting over after my fears crept into the novel's plot. I spent ever more time with Hudson and Lord Baruk riding both every afternoon in the arena and crying on Hudson's shoulder. "What should I do Hud?" Wait, I heard in my mind. "Okay, I will."

In the evening, I cooked and ate alone, and then ate Marshall's portion the next day for lunch. I'd finish the day with another cup of tea and buried in another book. Despite Marshall's occasional visits, I became fatalistic. If he backs out, I will survive, became the chant choked through sobs. I called Hannah and confessed my fears.

She encouraged me to give him the space but expect everything to go as planned.

"Don't worry until you have something to worry about."

I succumbed to my fears one evening and called to tell Marshall that I missed him and hoped he was okay. It had only been three days since his last visit. Would he consider that clinging?

I drove Sophie to Sidney's place the evening of the nineteenth as originally planned, being sure to keep a smile on my face. The morning of my wedding was still grey with huge thunderclouds rolling across the sky threatening more snow. The temperature hovered at thirty degrees which felt pretty mild compared to the lower twenties we'd had for most of March. I wasn't happy that the wind had kicked up, however.

Hannah, Dee Dee, and Sidney arrived to help me gather my things. In a moment of privacy I asked Hannah when I should start worrying?

She answered with a twinkle in her eye, "When you're walking down the aisle and he isn't waiting at the alter."

As I locked the door I wondered if I'd be returning as a married woman. During the drive into town, we joked about wasting money on getting our hair done when the wind was sure to dislike the effort and rearrange it for us. At some point during our hair appointment, I realized Dee Dee and Sidney were laughing and talking to me.

"You aren't getting cold feet are you?"

I could honestly answer, "No, but I am nervous."

Hannah gave me an encouraging wink.

Dee Dee dropped us as close to the door as possible saying her spikes would reassemble easier than our longer tresses. Hannah stayed with me as long as possible but then went to take her seat with mom and Dee Dee. Sidney's dark ringlets looked nice against her pale yellow, Swiss dot dress. The short sleeves were half caps. Her bouquet was yellow narcissus and white daffodil. I looked at my own bouquet of white roses and yellow narcissus and wondered if I'd get to throw them to an eager woman longing for matrimony.

We had decided against using 'Here Comes the Bride' as our entrance music. As I heard the first bars of the spring movement of Vivaldi's Four Seasons, I felt the color drain from my face. My fingers turned to ice and my knees to jelly. Sidney, misreading my agony, took my arm to lead me into the foyer where Dad waited to walk me down the aisle.

The door opened, the people stood as Sidney began her journey down the aisle. It wasn't a large wedding and most of the guests were on the groom's side. I couldn't see the front. I looked at faces for signs of worry. The preacher was smiling. Mom, Hannah and Dee Dee were smiling. They wouldn't be if Marshall wasn't in his place, I told myself. And then as I neared the front, he came into view. He was looking up at the ceiling, a frown on his face. I saw Connor nudge him with an elbow. He dropped his eyes to me. Our eyes locked. The frown dropped away. His dark eyes lit up and a smile followed. I could have sworn the sun came out at just that moment.

CHAPTER TWENTY-FOUR

Hawaii was wonderful. We swam in blue waters and lay on white-sanded beaches until our skin glowed coppery brown. We hiked through lush foliage, descended into slumbering volcanoes dreaming of their next opportunity to flex their muscles. We attended luaus and attempted to surf. Marshall shot roll after roll of exotic birds and blossoms. By the tenth day, it was harder to lie still on the warm sands. My mind kept thinking of the next chapter of my book; wondering how Sharla was doing and even with some anxiety, about the three girls waiting for me in saddle club.

Shelly had offered to supervise the saddle club girls for the two weeks we were away and I was wondering if she had been able to get 'the bubble' to focus. Her name was Bambi, and that wasn't the only problem. She didn't seem to be able to pay attention long enough to do a good job of grooming her horse, Polly. She even had trouble sitting still once she was in the saddle. Polly was starting to react by nipping or tuning out the spastic child. The other children were starting to complain and say mean things to her, causing her to cry. I hated having to give so much of the lesson time to Bambi. It wasn't fair to the other girls. I was desperately hoping Shelly had made some progress with her or found other sponsors to give the girls individual attention.

I could tell Marshall was getting fidgety as well. Over dinner one evening I asked, "It's about time to go home, isn't it?"

He grinned sheepishly. "This is probably the longest vacation I've ever had."

"Me too. I've loved every minute of it but I'm itching to get back to the novel, and I'm missing Hudson, Baruk and Sophie."

"Yeah. I've got some photo shoots lined up for when I get back. I keep thinking of where a good spot would be."

"We should design an outside area that would be a natural photo area for your outside shots. We could face it so the light is just right. Or create several so one side is right no matter what time of day it is. Put in foliage that is pretty in each season. Some rocks to sit on or a split rail fence to lean on. And we should use one of the rooms for indoor shoots during inclement weather."

"Jules, that's a great idea. Thank you."

"You're welcome. Marshall, may I ask what was going on just before the wedding?"

Marshall leaned in and gave me a gentle kiss. "I was scared spit less."

I laughed with relief. "I was so afraid you didn't love me anymore."

"I knew I loved you. I was just afraid of how marriage would change us and our relationship. I was angry at myself for proposing. Connor kept telling me the secret was commitment. When I saw you walking down the aisle with that worried look on your face; in an instant I realized what I had put you through those past few weeks. It literally felt like a knife in my heart. But even though I had hurt you, there you were, willing to start a life with me. That's when I knew I was taking a step I was meant to take."

"I'm glad you took it."

"So am I. I hope you'll always be glad you showed up."

"I have to admit I thought I'd feel like I had arrived at an apogee and would live in bliss ever after, but I'm already restless."

"It's time to take up our lives again."

"You know we are so blessed to be living lives we love. Not many people can say that."

"You're right, so let's not take it for granted, and give some back."

"Like working with the saddle club kids?"
"Yep."

When Marshall told me how Cody ran to him and gave him a hug at saddle club, it touched my heart. We really were important to these kids. Unfortunately, it didn't calm my jitters about my own session which would be on the following Wednesday.

I spent time with Hudson and Baruk but my mind was on Bambi and how I could get her to focus. As I was grooming Hudson, he started swinging his hindquarters back and forth between the stalls on either side of where he was cross tied, his hoofs clomping on the cement aisle. He stepped forward, and backed, and stepped forward again.

"Hudson, what is the matter with you?" I asked bringing my attention back to him.

I ran my hands along his neck pinching his crest and withers. He stopped immediately and swung his head to look at me. I returned his gaze and then smiled. "I get it."

Marshall wasn't home yet when I left for saddle club but he called to wish me luck. Shelly stuck her head out her office door and waved me over as soon as I pulled in.

"Please tell me you got more sponsors," I begged.

"I did. Two in fact, but only on the condition that they could each have someone other than Bambi." She paused watching my face.

I felt relief that I wouldn't have to juggle three. Despite Hudson giving me the key, I still felt disappointment that the one I was stuck with was Bambi. And then I felt sadness that no one wanted her, not even Polly, her mount. I smiled. "That's fine."

I saw Shelly release the breath she was holding. "The van is pulling in now."

"We may not make it to the arena this evening."

Shelly looked askance at me.

"I think she needs more than a horse. Maybe we'll get as far as grooming this evening."

"Do what you think you have to do. I certainly can't fault your tactics after seeing how you helped Sharla."

As the van came to a stop I was along side it. There was Bambi's face, staring glumly out the window, eyes red from crying. She didn't look at me; waited until everyone else was out of the vehicle before she followed.

"Hello Bambi. Are you ready to get to know each other? We didn't have much opportunity before, did we?"

Still looking at the ground, she shook her head no.

"Let's go up in the hay loft, okay?"

Bambi's eyes opened wide as she looked up at me. "Really?"

"Yeah. Let's go."

We climbed the ladder and rearranged some of the bales to create an enclosure.

"So how was your day at school?"

"Horrible."

"Why?"

"The teacher is always yelling at me to be quiet."

"You like to talk?"

Bambi picked at a bale of hay until she pulled loose a stem of Timothy and proceeded to pull it apart.

"Doesn't this hay smell good?" I asked.

She glanced at me as she answered and saw I was looking directly at her. She smiled. "Yes."

"Do you think the horses like the smell?"

"DUH." Bambi giggled. "Like we like the smell of chicken cooking."

"Oh yes, I like the smell of chicken cooking. Is that your favorite food?"

"Chicken and mashed potatoes with gravy. Mmmmm." Bambi rolled her eyes.

"Do you help your mom cook?"

She looked back at me and seemed startled to see I was still looking at her. "No. She says I talk too much. I get sent to my room a lot."

"What do you do in your room?"

"I color, or draw, or read."

I saw tears fill her eyes as she glanced away and my heart went out to her. "Do you play with dolls?"

"Sometimes."

"What kind of doll do you have?"

"She's old. Her hair is all messed up and her dress is old."

"What kind of doll would you like to have?"

"A baby doll."

"You mean one that wets itself and cries."

She nodded vigorously.

"Why?"

"So I can take care of it and it won't tell me to get lost."

"Who tells you to get lost?"

"Daddy. He's always watching football or basketball and if I talk he says, 'Get lost chatterbox'."

"Why do you talk so much in school? Don't you want to learn what the teacher is saying?"

"Yes, but I guess I want to talk to my friends more."

"Can't you talk to them at recess?"

She rolled her eyes away again. "They run away from me."

I moved closer to her and put my arm around her shoulders. "I would feel very hurt if someone did that to me."

Bambi made no answer but I heard a sniff.

"Are you ready to groom Polly?"

She looked up at me with tears still in her eyes. I held her gaze and wanted to cry with her when she said, "Polly doesn't like me either."

I forced a smile past the lump in my throat. "Well, why don't we go see if we can change that."

"How?"

"Let's go give it a try."

"Give what a try?"

175

"Come and find out."

At Polly's stall, I said, "Say hello to Polly and then I want you to be very quiet while you put on her halter and lead her to the grooming bay."

"Hello Polly."

Polly pinned her ears and Bambi looked at me. I looked into her eyes and kept a smile on my face. She turned back to her task in silence. Once Polly was in the cross ties, I went to Bambi's side.

"Now, without speaking human talk, we're going to speak horse talk to Polly."

Bambi's head spun to face me. "How?" she practically shouted.

Polly stamped a hoof, pinned her ears and backed away as far as the ties would allow her.

I put a finger to my lips. "Shh. Take your finger and thumb and pinch here on Polly's withers. That's horse talk for 'I want to make you feel good'. Now get your brushes. Start at the poll and work your way down. Don't do the legs until you're done with the body and use the soft brush from the knees down."

I had to keep backing Bambi's hands and brushes back to spots she glossed over. Whenever she looked up at me, I met her eyes. She'd smile and go back to work. As we were finishing picking the hoofs, someone yelled, "Saddle club van is loading"

Bambi looked at me sorrowfully. "I didn't get to ride."

I gave her a hug. "There's more to being a horsewoman than just riding, Bambi. It's also learning to care for, and gaining the respect of your horse. So for a couple weeks we're just going to get to know each other and learn to speak to Polly in her language. Did you notice she didn't nip at you today?"

Her eyes and mouth rounded in wonder.

"We're making progress already. So I'll see you next Wednesday."

I watched her get on the bus and take her seat by the window. No one sat with her but when she looked out the window, I was looking at her. She smiled and waved good-bye. As I got into my car, I whispered, "Thank you Hudson."

Putting the Stratus into gear, I smiled to myself. So I hadn't arrived anywhere except at the end of a chapter in my life. I had two fantastic horses, a loving husband, and I had rediscovered a family. Now it was time to turn the page. Face a pure, plain sheet of life to fill in anyway I pleased. What more could I want?

WHAT PEOPLE ARE SAYING ABOUT HOOF BEATS:

"I loved it...I'm saving it for my daughters...."
    Kristin Barr R.N.
    North Canton, OH.

"From the first moment on, It's fascinating."
    Sylvia Oberwahrenbrock
    Hagen, Germany

"A fantastic read! A great book all animal lovers will enjoy."
    Eunelda Andrews R.N.
    Beach City, OH.

"You had me in tears, you had me laughing, you had me experiencing empathy, frustration, aggravation, the hope when Madison felt the stirrings of love in her heart...."
    Lynn Emery, member of Passionate Readers book club, Yakima, WA.

To order books by Rae D'Arcy, send money order for twelve dollars plus two dollars for shipping to:
    Darcy E. Miller
    P.O. Box 32
    Maximo, Oh. 44650-0032

Jewel Fitzgerald is starting over; minus a husband and the confidence and self esteem he demolished; facing an empty apartment and a horse she hadn't bargained for. It isn't long before the skeletons start knocking from the closet and dance back into her life in rapid succession; the steps taking her back and forward.